"It's not every day that you tell me you want to get married and get pregnant," Jack said.

Beth nestled her body against his. "Jack, I'm going to need your help with this one. I can't do it alone."

"You know you can always count on me. I'm your best friend, remember? Don't we always help each other?"

She nodded.

"Then what can I do to help you?" he asked.

Beth licked her lips. "Well, Jack…it's really quite simple. I need *you* to marry me and get me pregnant.…"

Kristin Morgan lives in Lafayette, Louisiana, the best heart of Acadiana, where the French language of her ancestors is still spoken fluently by her parents and grandparents. Happily married to her childhood sweetheart, she has three children. In addition to her writing, she enjoys cooking and preparing authentic Cajun food for her family with recipes passed on to her through generations. Her hobbies include reading—of course!—travelling, flower gardening and fishing. She loves walking in the rain, newborn babies, all kinds of music, chocolate desserts and love stories with happy endings. A true romantic at heart, she believes all things are possible with love.

SHOTGUN GROOM

BY
KRISTIN MORGAN

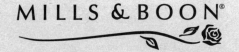

MILLS & BOON®

*First published in Great Britain 2001
Harlequin Mills & Boon Limited,
Eton House, 18-24 Paradise Road, Richmond, Surrey TW9 1SR*

© Barbara Lantier Veillon 1998

ISBN 0 263 82642 2

*Set in Times Roman 10½ on 12¼ pt.
02-0102-44224*

*Printed and bound in Spain
by Litografia Rosés, S.A., Barcelona*

Chapter One

Thirty-four-year-old Bethemy Trahan needed a sperm donor.

But not just any old sperm donor. Uh-uh. No way. Not for her baby.

It had to be someone she knew and cared for. Someone who would be willing to marry her temporarily and get the job done in the good, old-fashioned way that couples had used since the beginning of time. She was, after all, a traditional-minded woman. She couldn't just make use of a sperm bank and then have an illegitimate baby, no matter how much she wanted a child of her own. It went against everything she had ever planned for herself. She had to get married first, then get pregnant.

But since Mr. Right had put a major damper on her plans by failing to show up in her life, Beth had recently decided that it was time she took matters into her own hands. A daunting fact she could no longer ignore was that her mother had gone through menopause at the young age of thirty-seven. There was always the chance that Beth would, too. Time, she knew, was very possibly running out for her. No more could she rely solely on Fate to get the job done.

But then, she really didn't have to. She was lucky. She wasn't going to have to depend on the laboratory-like coldness of a sperm bank. She had an alternative. She had Jack Kincaid. He was her oldest and dearest friend in the whole wide world. Without question, he was the perfect specimen for what she had in mind. He had a great set of genes. He was intelligent, handsome, funny—the very best friend a girl could ask for. The fact that he *was* her best friend and was sometimes—well, more often than not—easy to convince to her way of thinking was only extra pudding in the pie. A bit of *lapniappe*. In fact, Beth had no earthly idea why she hadn't thought of marrying him a long time ago for the sole purpose of getting pregnant.

Of course, as of yet, Jack was oblivious to all of this. He had no idea of the plan she'd recently come up with. In fact, his job as a sales representative for a Louisiana based food export company had taken him abroad to Europe for the past two weeks. But he was back home now, and he was coming over for dinner at her house later that evening. She planned to tell him then. Undoubtedly he was going to be surprised at her news. Somewhat shocked, even. Actually Beth was still a bit dazzled herself over the plan she'd concocted. Naturally she was anxious to get the moment behind her.

Well…on second thought, she was more than just anxious. She was scared silly of what she had in mind—or, at least, a part of her was. The last thing she wanted under any circumstance was to jeopardize the long-standing relationship she already had with Jack. His friendship was too important to her. Too necessary. And too much of the time she needed him to be there for her. He had been her best pal since first grade. Since the day she tore the pretty new dress she had just gotten for her birthday while playing hopscotch at recess and he'd given her a piece of his candy bar to stop her from crying. On that day, a unique bond had formed between them and just the thought of losing even a small portion of what they shared caused Beth unbearable distress.

Then again, there was no reason why her recent idea should jeopardize her and Jack's present relationship. Not if she had planned it accurately.

And, of course, she had. She always planned accurately. According to Jack, sometimes to a fault.

In fact, it was her ability to work out the details of an idea that made this new plan of hers so stunningly brilliant. Jack's involvement was going to be so minimal, there wouldn't be enough time to jeopardize anything—certainly, not enough time for them to, let's say, accidentally fall in love with each other and ruin everything. She knew the result of letting something like that happen between friends. Her own parents were a good example. Married once, but now divorced, their behavior these days suggested that they hated each other, and Beth wasn't so sure that wasn't the case. Thanks, but no thanks. That wasn't the unhappy ending she wanted for herself and Jack. His friendship meant too much to her.

Short and quick. In and out. No time—or plans, for that matter—for falling in love. That was the name of her game. Besides, how long could it take for a virile guy like Jack to get her pregnant? Two months tops, right?

Maybe less.

The thought of it made her stomach quiver.

And as soon as she found out that she was pregnant, they would get a divorce and their lives would return to normal. Jack could go back to his single, carefree life-style, and she would have her baby. It was a perfect plan. Absolutely perfect.

At least, she thought so.

Karen was a different matter.

A close friend who had just dropped in for a brief visit, Karen now gazed at her from across the kitchen as if she had just grown two heads. "Are you crazy, Beth? Jack is never going to go for an idea like that. Not in a million years. Not even for you."

"I know it sounds a bit wild," Beth said hesitantly, wondering if all her friends—including Jack—were going to feel the same way about her idea. Her heart began pounding in her throat. Jack was her last hope. He was the only man she felt she could ask to father her child. If he said no…

The truth was, he was the *only* man she wanted to ask. Now that she'd come up with this plan, the idea of having his baby was...well...comforting. Somehow, it fit. He was her friend, after all. They were like two peas in a pod. But what if, like Karen, he thought she'd gone off the deep end and refused to help her, deciding, instead to have her institutionalized for treatment. How was he ever going to get her pregnant while she was locked in a padded cell?

Realizing how weird her thoughts had become, Beth shook her head. Okay, so she was losing it, somewhat. It was her nerves, she knew. They were strung out like barbed wire, and Karen's disapproving looks from across her kitchen certainly weren't helping matters. "I'm going to ask him anyway," Beth stated with renewed conviction, placing the green salad she'd just made inside the refrigerator.

"Fine. Be my guest," Karen exclaimed. "But if you get your feelings crushed, don't say I didn't warn you."

"I consider myself warned," Beth replied flatly.

"You're barking up the wrong tree. Jack will never go for it," Karen said in a singsong voice.

"He might."

"Not our Jack. He's the last man on earth who wants to get married—for any reason. You, of all people, should know that about him."

"I do. I'm simply hoping I can talk him into it."

"Well, I must admit," Karen said nonchalantly, "if anyone can talk him into something as wild and crazy as this, no doubt about it, it's you. He'll listen to anything you have to say." She paused with a smirk. "He isn't that open-minded when it comes to listening to the rest of us."

"You're forgetting something important, Karen. Jack and I have been friends since we were kids. Of course he listens to what I have to say." She smiled knowingly. "In fact, he knows he had better."

"Yeah, yeah, I've heard that old story before," Karen said with a wave of her hand. "How the two of you have been friends since grade school. But in spite of what you say, I've come to the conclusion that there's much more to this 'Beth and Jack thing' than either of you will ever admit."

"Well, you're wrong," Beth said. "Jack and I both freely admit that we have a very special friendship. But that's it—period."

Karen rolled her eyes. "Yeah, right."

Beth frowned in frustration. She hated it when she had to defend her relationship with Jack to their friends. So it lacked any sexual undertones—why was that so difficult for everyone to understand? This was the nineties, for heaven's sake. Surely there were plenty of other men and women who shared a special bond that had nothing whatsoever to do with their crawling into bed together. Their friends needed to wake up and smell the variety of coffee out there on the market today. Times had changed, and Beth was proud in knowing that she and Jack were an intricate part of that change. If only some of their friends were so enlightened.

"Look, Karen," Beth said a moment later, "if

what you believe about Jack and me is so true, then what about his little black book?''

Karen shrugged. ''What about it?''

''Well, if what you're trying to imply is true, why does he carry one around with him? And why doesn't it bother me?''

Once more, Karen shrugged. ''Beats me. As far as I can see, nothing's standard procedure when it comes to the two of you.'' Stopping short, she tilted her head to the side and peered thoughtfully at Beth. ''By the way, since you've brought up the subject of Jack's little black book…have you ever seen him actually use it?''

''Of course, I have. Lots of times,'' Beth replied, without the slightest hesitation. After giving herself another moment to think about it, she pulled her eyebrows into a frown. Or had she?

Of course she had, she told herself a second later. Plenty of times. At the moment, she just couldn't recall a particular incident where that was true. Given time, she most certainly would. It was just that Karen had her under the gun and, therefore, her brain was scrambled. ''Karen, I really don't have time right now to discuss this with you. Jack's coming over soon. So could we please drop the subject?''

''Sure,'' Karen replied coolly.

Taking a deep breath, Beth forced a smile. ''Thank you.''

Hoping that the subject was now officially closed, at least for the time being, Beth began bustling around her brightly lit kitchen, mentally checking off the last-minute things she had to do before Jack would arrive for the gourmet dinner she had planned for them later that night. All the while, though, her stomach was in knots. She wanted this night to be perfect. She had bought Jack's favorite wine…prepared his favorite foods…and had put his favorite music in the CD player.

The mood was set. No matter what anyone else thought, her plan *was* a good one. It could work. It *would* work.

It was all up to Jack now.

Everything—her hopes, her dreams—was banking on her ability to convince Jack that she needed his help. Badly. Desperately. He'd never let her down before. Never. Without question, if anyone could help her, it was Jack.

Beth set a vase of fresh spring flowers from the florist at the center of the linen-draped table she had set, then stepped back and studied it.

Standing nearby, Karen began shaking her head from side to side. "Poor guy. Jack is going to be walking head-on into a trap and he doesn't even have the slightest clue."

Ignoring her friend's comment, Beth frowned thoughtfully as she stepped back a few feet more and carefully inspected the table. "Does it look to you like I've covered everything?"

Karen gazed at the formal setting and then shrugged. "As far as I can tell, everything but the kitchen sink."

Deepening her frown, Beth looked up at her friend.

"In all honesty, Karen, do you think there's even the slightest chance that Jack will turn me down?"

It took Karen a moment to answer, but finally she broke into a reassuring smile. "Look, don't mind me, honey. I was just being an old fuddy-duddy earlier. If this is what you think you need to do, then go for it."

"Oh, Karen," Beth said, grabbing her friend's hands and holding onto them for a moment. "Thanks for understanding."

Karen's smile warmed even more. "Sometimes it's a real challenge to keep up with you, Beth, but I'm trying. In any case, you can take what I'm about to tell you with a grain of salt, but it's true nonetheless. When Jack arrives, if you just bat those big brown eyes of yours at him like this—" she demonstrated the technique with her own eyes "—he won't stand a chance. I've seen it happen before. He's putty in your hands when you look at him like that."

"Really?" Beth asked, her dark eyes widening in surprise. "I never noticed."

"Of course you haven't. You're too busy making sure that everyone knows that you're simply his best buddy—and *not* his love interest."

Beth gave her friend a mild glare. "Karen…"

"Okay, okay. I'm finished. In fact, now that I've had a moment, I think you're right. Jack is the perfect choice to father your child."

Beth released a deep sigh. "Well now," she said, "see how easy that was."

"I'm only changing my mind because I'm hoping

that this plan of yours will somehow wake up at least one of you to the truth,'' Karen replied. ''Otherwise, it looks to me like you two may very well end up going through life as nothing more than friends.''

''Actually that's exactly what Jack and I plan to do,'' Beth said stubbornly.

Suddenly Karen glanced down at her wristwatch and gaped. ''Good grief, would you look at the time? I've got to scoot. Beth, don't forget about the party tomorrow night at my house. And remind Jack of it, too, will you?''

''I will,'' Beth replied.

Karen turned abruptly, like a wasp that was suddenly honed in on its prey, and headed for the door. ''The dry cleaner down the street closes in fifteen minutes and I won't have a thing to wear tomorrow if I don't get there in time to pick up my clothes,'' she said, swiping up her leather purse from the kitchen counter.

Beth followed her friend to the door, a nagging thought from their earlier discussion still on her mind. Suddenly it seemed vitally important to Beth that Karen understand her plan wasn't going to change anything between herself and Jack. At this point, the last thing she needed was a misunderstanding with Karen. If that were to happen, undoubtedly it would quickly spread like wildfire among their friends. ''Karen, listen to me,'' Beth said. ''I don't want you getting ideas about me and Jack that are simply not true. Nothing has changed. Jack and I are friends—period.

''Besides,'' she quickly added, ''as one of my clos-

est friends, you know how I feel. Under no circumstance will I jeopardize the relationship that Jack and
I already have, not even if I had a written guarantee
of improving it. Frankly I don't think it can be im-
proved. It's perfect, just as it is. Besides, in the long
run we'd be taking the chance of ruining everything
we have. My parents did, remember? Their marriage
ruined their friendship. They became different people.
Eventually they fell out of love.'' Beth held her chin
slightly higher. ''The problem is, some people refuse
to acknowledge that Jack and I will never let that
happen to us. If and when I ever fall in love, it will
be with someone other than Jack, of that much you
can be sure. And as far as Jack is concerned, he says
he is never going to fall in love. And those, Karen,
are the facts.''

''You know something, Beth,'' Karen said, turning
to face her, ''if what you're looking for in life is
guarantees, I've got news for you. You're not going
to get them—no matter how many precautions you
take. Sooner or later, you'll have to take that bungy
jump into life just like the rest of us. After that, it's
up to Fate.''

''Uh-uh,'' Beth replied with a shake of her head.
''Not me. I plan ahead, every step of the way.''

Karen frowned at her for a moment and then turned
for the door. ''Look, honey, I gotta run. But in spite
of all I've just said to you, I'll have my fingers
crossed the entire night that everything goes according to your plan. Just hit Jack with everything you've
got, and I know you'll win him over to your way of

thinking. You always do.'' Then she shot out the door like a streak of lightning in her hot pink dress and matching heels.

After her friend left, Beth pivoted on her heels and started down the hall in the direction of her bedroom. She felt stressed-out from the conversation she'd just had and wondered how Karen could be so adamantly wrong about her and Jack's friendship. Beth saw no reason why anyone should have a problem with it.

Pausing momentarily, she took a deep, steadying breath. Right now she had other, more important things to worry about. First of all, it was time she got moving. Jack would be arriving at her door any minute. She needed to take one final glance at herself in the mirror. Too much was at stake for her to overlook even the slightest detail that might make a difference. The more carefully she planned, the more positive would be her results. She believed that wholeheartedly.

But, in truth, she had an ulterior motive for wanting to study her reflection in the mirror one final time. Now that Karen had mentioned it, she decided it wouldn't hurt to practice batting her eyes in the manner that her friend had suggested. Just in case. Who knew what it would take to sway Jack over to her way of thinking? Maybe the eyes would do it.

Not that she honestly believed that it would. Again, her nerves were intervening with her common sense. If anything, she knew without a doubt that Jack wasn't attracted to her in a romantic way. Nor was she attracted to him like that. Oh sure, she was willing to admit that she'd noticed he had a great pair of buns. But that certainly didn't mean anything. Most women noticed that about Jack. They noticed a lot of other things, too. Like his sexy smile and his sometimes cocky manner. With light brown hair, blue eyes and a squared-off jaw that gave his face added prominence—and, of course, just a hint of arrogance—he had a look about him that grabbed the attention of the opposite sex. He had a great body, not to mention a resonant voice that was as deep and rich as chicory-blended coffee. He wasn't Cajun by heritage, not like she was. Nonetheless, his Irish roots harmonized well with the French Acadian culture that was so prevalent in south Louisiana. They both adored the joie de vivre that had been handed down by her French ancestors as a way of life. They liked the same music, the same spicy Cajun foods. They even liked to hang out with the same people. He was her best buddy in all the ways that mattered, and she loved him dearly because of it.

But when someone tried to imply that there was something more than a special bond of friendship between them, it really bothered her. In fact, it had been known to keep her awake nights, just worrying about it.

And it frightened her, too.

Heaven knew, she needed Jack in her life too much to ever consider letting herself fall in love with him.

Jack Kincaid was glad to be back in town. He liked it okay when he had to travel abroad on business, but it was always great to get back home and relax in the company of his friends.

In fact, he was going over to Beth's house tonight. She'd invited him for dinner when he'd called earlier to tell her that he was back. He couldn't wait to see her. Of all his immediate friends, she was the one whom he missed the most when he was away on business. Of course, there was a perfectly good reason for that. With Beth, he never had to worry about his next move. He could tune out the rest of the world and just be himself. With her, he didn't have to pretend to have all the answers. She was his sounding board. His best buddy. She was the kind of person who could bring him to his knees and make him face the truth about himself faster than anyone else. Still, he always felt at ease when in her company. And, truthfully, there wasn't another female alive whom he could say that about.

He was a lucky man, all right, to have Beth there for him when he needed a pal. He was, in fact, perfectly content with his single way of life, and had no problem admitting that in many ways he had Beth to thank for that. He only wished that she was as pleased with the way her life was turning out. But she wasn't and lately he could almost sense her discontent. If only the man of her dreams would finally come along so she could get married and then get pregnant with that baby she was always wanting. It was disconsoling that her life hadn't worked out exactly as she'd planned. Even more unfortunate was that he couldn't help her, no matter how good a friend he was. It was

Mother Nature's call—not his—to attract the right man to Beth. He was just someone whose shoulder she could cry on time and time again when it didn't happen.

If it was up to him, he would see to it that Beth got what she wanted most in life. There wasn't a doubt in his mind that his friend would make the best mamma any little kid ever had.

With that thought still on his mind, Jack pulled up in front of Beth's house. He saw that her porch light was on, and it beckoned to him like a friendly greeting as he climbed out of his car with a sense of urgency. With a grin on his face and a swelling in his chest, he headed for her front door.

It had been two long weeks since he'd seen Beth last. It was a long time for him to have gone without his best pal in his life. A part of him needed her more than it needed nourishment.

Beth was in her living room when Jack drove up, and she watched his approach through the long window next to the door. He was wearing a pair of jeans and a navy pullover shirt. He looked great, just as he always did, and her heart began to pound erratically. It was always that way when she saw him coming from a distance. It was, she knew, the sensuous way his hips rolled forward when he walked that mesmerized her. Sometimes her heart seemed to roll right along with them. Sometimes her equilibrium did, too, although it was rare that she let herself recognize those particular feelings for what they really were. Usually she chose to ignore them altogether.

By the time Jack reached her porch, Beth had her hand on the knob and was pulling the front door open. He immediately waltzed inside with a grin on his face that for as long as she could remember had always had a way of melting her cares away, no matter how bad they had seemed before. Suddenly she was swept up into his arms and wrapped in one of his infamous bear hugs.

Bear hugs, Beth had come to realize a long time ago, were a safe way for them to express their feelings for each other. Bear hugs lacked…well…great passion. They were fun…friendly…acceptable.

"How's my favorite girl?" Jack asked, squeezing her tight against him. "Mmm… You know, it isn't until I get a whiff of your perfume that I know for sure that I'm home."

Beth was so glad to see him that her laughter bubbled out when he squeezed her.

And then, for some silly reason, her stomach went spiraling down to the floor. She quickly decided it was because she was so excited to see him. Certainly it was nothing more than that. He was her friend, for heaven's sake.

Ignoring the sensation, she wrapped her arms around his neck and hugged him as tight as she could. The light musky scent of his aftershave was as familiar to her as her own perfume and for a moment the combination of the two gave her a heady sensation.

His body was so hard...so solid.

His arms went around her waist.

Her stomach quivered.

Her world was back in town now, and everything was going to work out just as she had planned. She was sure of it.

"I cooked your favorite dinner," she said, smiling up at him.

He grinned down at her with his wide, full lips. Lips that were perfect for grinning.

And for kissing, no doubt.

Not that she knew for sure. She was only imagining what his lips would feel like pressed against hers. Hypothetically speaking, of course.

"So what's the occasion?" Jack asked. "Did I forget a holiday or something?"

"Nope," Beth replied, pleased as pudding with herself for having planned such a great evening. Motherhood was practically in the bag for her. All she had to do now was to convince Jack of just how important his help was to her. She widened her grin. "No particular reason. I just felt like making this night kind of special. Actually," she added, "I have a bottle of your favorite wine, too."

"Oh...?" he said, giving her a rather odd look. His grin faltered somewhat. "Beth, you haven't done it again, have you?"

She widened her eyes in response. "Done what?"

He narrowed his gaze. "You know what."

"No, I don't."

"Then you're obviously forgetting the last time I

came over to discover that you had cooked all my favorite foods for no particular reason. But we both know that in the end you did have a reason. You had volunteered my services as judge in that pie-tasting contest, remember? And do you remember what a catastrophe that turned out to be?''

Beth gave him a placative smile. ''Now look, Jack, that women's club was happy to have you as their judge…originally. In fact, for a time you had the entire membership charmed right down to their silver-dyed roots. It wasn't a catastrophe until you made it into one.''

''Me?'' he said, incredulously, placing his finger-tips at the center of his chest. ''I didn't do anything wrong. I simply picked a winner. Isn't that what a judge in any contest is supposed to do? How was I supposed to know that all those little old ladies were going to suddenly turn on me when I announced the winner and it turned out to be the same woman who had won the contest the previous year?''

''Jack, all those women were well into their seventies—some, probably, in their eighties. Most of them were great-great-grandmothers. They weren't exactly going to eat you alive.''

''Yeah, well, you can stand here and say that. It wasn't *you* they were aiming their dirty looks at. To this day, if I meet up with a couple of them in the supermarket, they won't even speak to me.''

In spite of the serious discussion she had planned for later that night, Beth laughed at Jack's recollection of that particular afternoon. Thank goodness, she had gone with him to help with the contest. Otherwise, he would have panicked for sure. As it was, he had vowed never to sit in judgment of another woman's cooking for as long as he lived. "It wasn't that bad, Jack."

He placed his hands on his hips. "Look, I like little old ladies as much as anyone, but please tell me that you haven't volunteered my services to them again."

"No, Jack, I haven't," Beth said prudently, suffering from a moment of slight indignation. After all, she'd only volunteered his name to the Retired Women's Business Club of Acadiana because he'd said he wanted to get more actively involved with the community. And regardless of what he thought now, he was a better citizen today because of it. "It's nothing like that. Besides, it just so happens that the committee chairperson this year didn't ask me to find a judge for the contest."

That remark seemed to fly right past Jack as he gazed at her. "Okay," he said, "if it isn't another contest, then what is it?"

Surprised that he was on to her so easily—she had honestly thought she'd been doing such a great job at hiding her emotions—Beth paused momentarily to regroup. "Uh... It can wait until after we have dinner."

Jack narrowed his eyes in concern. "I don't think so. You've made it sound too serious for that."

Beth cleared her throat. "Look, it's no big deal. Certainly it isn't anything that you're probably imagining," she said, hoping to somehow stall him for as long as she could. She simply wasn't ready to tell him about her idea. Besides, she had a wonderful evening planned for them. If she got lucky, by the end of it Jack would be willing to help her with her dilemma. But if she jumped the gun on everything and told him her plan now, there was no telling what might happen. The truth was, she liked to stick to a game plan. It made her life predictable...stable.

Beth glanced up and found Jack frowning at her. "Frankly, Beth," he said, "I don't know what to think. Are you sick or something?"

"No," she said, giving her head a hardy shake.

"Are you in some kind of trouble?"

"No, of course not."

"Well, that's a relief," Jack said. Then he deepened his frown. "Look, whatever it is, it can't be that bad. I'm here now, I can help."

Suddenly tears sprang to Beth's eyes. "Oh, Jack, I knew I could count on you," she said.

Taking her by the shoulders, Jack looked deep into her eyes. "Of course, you can count on me," he said, giving her a reassuring smile. "So stop worrying. Everything is going to be just fine."

Somehow, Beth managed to give him the smile she knew he wanted from her. "As a matter of fact, it's starting to look that way already," she said, suddenly experiencing a wave of deep, unbridled emotion. Emotion that had suddenly taken a detour from its normal path and was now channeling its way through her heart. She loved this guy more than anyone else in the whole world. So why shouldn't her feelings for him come straight from her heart? She pressed her body against his and for a brief moment reveled in the comforting thought that he was near. "And it's all because of you, Jack." Gazing up at him with wide, soulful eyes, she gave him the brightest smile she could possibly muster under the circumstances.

A silly-looking grin slipped up one side of his face. "See," he said teasingly, landing a playful blow to the side of her jaw. "Your Knight in Shining Armor has arrived. He's just packaged differently than you thought he would be."

Beth was captivated by the thought. But she quickly reminded herself that she had strict rules of conduct against such things happening between them. For heaven's sake, Jack couldn't be her Knight in Shining Armor. He was her best friend.

With that in mind, she shoved aside her disturbing thoughts and forced herself to laugh out loud—which, needless to say, was as much for her benefit as it was for his. "Yeah, right," she said, teasing him back.

Widening his grin, he glanced over his shoulder as though in search of something. "Well, I don't see anyone else lined up for the job. I guess I'm all you've got—at least for the time being. You know the old saying," he said laughingly. "Beggars can't be choosers."

Beth was smiling at Jack's silly attempt to make her laugh when suddenly she sobered, reminding herself of what she had planned. "Oh, Jack, this is no laughing matter. This is one time I'm in desperate need of your help."

Placing his hands on his hips, Jack came to an immediately standstill. "Okay, Beth," he said, with a slow shake of his head. "I can't take any more of this. I need to know what's going on here. It's time you level with me."

Beth was trembling on the inside. Clearly it seemed her moment of truth had arrived. "I want a baby, Jack."

Chapter Two

Suddenly Beth found herself at a loss. Now that her carefully laid plan for a perfect evening with Jack was lying in shambles at her feet, she didn't know where to begin her story. She hated when something she had planned so meticulously went haywire. She felt stripped of her confidence, and her stomach was in knots.

After taking in some badly needed oxygen, she suddenly found herself wondering how she was ever going to explain in no uncertain terms to her very best friend in the whole wide world that she wanted him to compromise a small portion of his future for the sake of her own.

In that moment she wondered how she—or anyone—could even think of being so selfish.

But then, in almost the next second, the thought of

never having her very own child shrouded over her like a cloud of doom, making her feel sick to her stomach and more than ready to do just about anything to have that one goal in her life come true.

Oh, God, wouldn't it be all right if she asked Jack to do her just this one, big favor?

Besides, if he didn't want to, all he had to do was say no. She would accept that. She would have to.

Taking a deep breath, Beth mentally prepared herself for the battle ahead. "Jack, you know, of course, how I've always said I wanted to have a child of my own."

Keeping his hands placed on his hips, he gave her a hesitant grin. "Sure," he said. "It's been your dream in life since…well…since forever. Why?"

"I'm not getting any younger, and that dream still isn't a reality. Therefore, I've decided to take matters into my own hands," she continued, pausing briefly for a breath. "I've come up with this terrific plan—"

Jack rolled his eyes. "Oh, no. Not another one of your plans. I knew it. I bet it involves me, right?"

His abrupt manner stunned Beth and she looked him square in the face. Finally, in a voice held tight with emotion, she said, "Yes. You could say that."

"I knew it," he exclaimed. "I knew the moment I walked through your front door that you had me involved in something. What is it this time?" he asked. He seemed so proud of himself for having been one step ahead of her.

Beth couldn't really blame him for being so skeptical of her motives. Over the years her ideas had gotten him involved in some pretty wild schemes. But convincing him to let her tag along with him and his date the night of their senior prom when her own date had come down at the last minute with a bad case of poison ivy paled enormously in comparison to what she now had in mind for them. So did the time ten years ago when she'd convinced him to let her go along with him and a couple of other guys on a white-water rafting trip. She'd almost drowned them all—or so Jack had said at the time. All she'd done was accidentally knock one poor guy out of the boat, but they'd gotten him back inside right away. He had for-given her ages ago. It was time that Jack did, too.

Still, she grimaced at the thought that he was on to her already. "This time is different, Jack, really it is."

He had dropped his hands down to his sides, but he immediately brought them back up to his hips and gave her an impatient glance. "Okay, Beth, I'll take the bait. What exactly does *different* mean?"

Anyone else would have probably been intimidated by his cocky manner, but not Beth. In fact, she found herself following his movements and thinking of what nice hands he had. His palms were wide, his fingers long and lean and, of course, his nails were trimmed neatly. Knowing Jack as she did, she had little doubt that they were the kind of hands that were strong, yet gentle when he made love to a woman. She had al-ways secretly hoped that her Knight in Shining Armor would have hands like Jack.

She took a deep breath after swallowing the sudden lump in her throat. "I've decided I want to get pregnant."

"Pregnant?" he replied, dumbfounded. A moment later, he smirked. "You're kidding me right?"

"No, I'm not," she replied."

A stunned expression framed his face. Tucking his hands into the pockets of his jeans, he rocked back on his heels. "Jeez, Beth, when did you decide all this?"

"A couple of weeks ago. Right after you left town on business."

"Why didn't you tell me when I called the other night?"

Without meeting his eyes, Beth shrugged. "You were still overseas in France. It just didn't seem like the right time."

He ran his fingers through his hair. "This is rather sudden, don't you think? For heaven's sake, you're not even married."

"I know," Beth replied. "But I plan to remedy that. The fact is, Jack, whether or not you like my idea, I've already made up my mind to go through with it. I can't just sit back anymore and wait for Fate to take its course. I have to take charge of my life now, before it's too late."

"Okay," he said. "I can understand if you're feeling that way about your life. We all do at times. But some things in life just naturally take time."

"There's nothing natural about not having my

dreams come true. And as far as time is concerned, I'm quickly running out of it, even as we speak. I know I've already told you this before, but if I follow in my mother's and grandmother's footsteps, there's a good chance that I'm going to go through menopause at a young age. All I may have left are two—possibly, three—good years. I can't just allow those years to roll past me without even making an attempt to do something about it."

Jack stepped back and regarded her intently. "Look," he said, "I wish as much as you do that the guy of your dreams had shown up by now. But that doesn't mean that he won't. Who knows, he might be just around the next corner.

Beth gave him a dispassionate glare. "Come on, Jack, you know as well as I do that it's unlikely he'll ever show up in my life. And even if he were to show eventually, it would probably be too late by then for me to have my own child. I simply won't let that happen. That's where you come into my plan, Jack."

Jack took a step back. "Me?" he said, as though surprised. A moment later, an enlightened gleam settled in his eyes. "Oh, I get it," he said. "You need me to help you find a reputable sperm bank." He shook his head affirmatively. "Well, don't you worry about a thing. I'll take care of that part. If you're that determined to go through with this, it's the least I can do to help you out."

Beth swallowed the lump in her throat. "Jack, I'm not exactly planning to use a sperm bank."

It took him a moment, but after giving her an astounded-looking grin, he finally said, "I don't understand, Beth. Just how are you planning to get pregnant?"

Her heart began pounding with anticipation. "The good old-fashioned way."

Jack's grin widened. "What are you saying exactly?"

"I'm saying that I plan on getting pregnant by sleeping with a guy. Of course, he and I will have to get married first."

"What?" Jack said, pulling his shoulders back.

Before he could say anything more, Beth hurriedly cut in. "And then as soon as the job is done," she answered, "he and I will get a divorce. Sounds perfect, doesn't it?"

"Sounds crazy, you mean," Jack exclaimed in his next breath. "Beth, have you lost your mind?"

Beth licked her lips. She had known this wasn't going to be easy. "I know it sounds crazy. Karen already told me as much. But, frankly, it makes perfectly good sense to me."

"Well, Karen's right," he said. "You can't do something like this."

"And why not?"

"Because…well…because it isn't like you."

"You know something," she exclaimed, placing her hands on her hips, "maybe I'm tired of being *like me*. Maybe I want to be different. Maybe I want to be someone who is willing to take a chance in order to get what she wants in life.''

Stepping forward, Jack took her by the shoulders. ''Look, honey, I think it's great that you feel that way. But do you have to take such a big, flying leap the first time out of the nest?''

Beth's bottom lip began to tremble. ''I don't expect you to understand,'' she said as tears sprang to her eyes. In truth, she had been expecting him to understand, and she couldn't even begin to acknowledge how disappointed she was that he obviously didn't.

''Hey, come on now,'' he said, pulling her against him. He was so solid…so dependable…so much what she needed right then in all aspects of the word. Why couldn't he see that? Especially since he already knew all there ever was to know about her.

Hugging her tight, Jack looked down at her and said, ''What's with all the tears? Look, I'm sorry if I said something to upset you. I'm just a little shook up by all of this, okay? It's not every day that you tell me you want to get married and get pregnant, all practically in the same breath. Give me a moment for it all to sink in.''

Beth nestled her body against his, savoring the warmth, the security of being as close to him as possible. He was her security blanket. Her shoulder to cry on. He knew her like no one else did. Finally, in spite of her desire to stay snuggled against him, she sucked up her tears and stepped back so she could gaze directly into his face.

"Jack, I'm really going to need your help with this one. I can't do it alone."

"Hey," he said, looking deep into her eyes. "You know you can always count on me. I'm your best friend, remember? Don't we always help each other?"

She nodded.

"Then what can I do to help you?" he asked point blank, suddenly cutting right through all the bull and getting to the heart of the matter.

Beth licked her lips again. "Well, Jack," she said, "it's really quite simple. I need you to marry me. I need to get pregnant."

His grin broadened momentarily, then wilted away in two seconds flat. In a grave tone of voice, he said, "You're joking, right?"

She shook her head. "No, I'm not. That's what I've been trying to tell you all along. I need you to father my baby."

Jack gaped at her.

"Look," she continued in a hurry, "before you give me your answer, let me just say one thing. There's no one else I feel I can trust with this. No matter what, I know I'll be safe with you, Jack."

"You can't be serious about this," he said.

"Oh, but I am," she replied.

"In that case, let me just say one thing. If you think I'm the guy for the job, you've lost your mind."

"I know I'm asking a lot—"

Taking a step back from her, Jack gave her a thawing glance. "You can say that again."

"Even though we're the best of friends, I really have some nerve putting you on the spot like this."

"You bet."

"You're right, you know," she said haughtily. "I should simply ask someone else, regardless of the consequences."

"Now wait a minute," he said, coming up straight. "I didn't say for you to do that." He ran his fingers through his hair, then paused for a long moment. "Jeez, Beth, do you have any idea what you're asking me to do?"

"Yes, I think so," she replied evenly. But her heart was pounding like mad. "Look, it's only for a temporary period of time."

Jack shook his head. "B-but I don't understand. What about all our years together as friends? You've always said—"

"I know what I've always said. And I haven't changed my mind about that," she replied, placing her hands flat against his chest and feeling the beating of his heart beneath her touch. "All I want is for us to get married and stay married only for as long as it takes to get me pregnant."

Once again, Jack stood, gaping at her. "In other words, Beth, because it now suits your purpose, it's okay for us to have sex together. Frankly, after all you've said over the years against such a thing ever happening between us, I'm floored that you would even consider doing it now—under any circumstances.''

Suddenly Beth's eyes filled with tears, and she realized in that moment that deep down inside she had been hoping all along that Jack wouldn't offer any resistance to her plan. That he would simply say yes right away and that would be the end of it. As it was, she didn't know if she had the stamina to continue trying to talk him into something as serious as fathering her child when he obviously didn't want any part of it.

She turned from him and plucked a tissue from a box on a nearby table, but she didn't have to use it after all. Miraculously she regained her composure.

By now, Jack had come up behind her and had placed his hands on her shoulders. ''Beth, let me make sure I'm getting this straight before I say any more. You want me—I mean *us* to have sex together for the sole purpose of getting you pregnant, right?''

Recognizing her last chance in convincing him to her way of thinking, Beth whirled to face him. ''Oh, Jack, yes, that's exactly what I mean. And as soon as I get pregnant, I promise, we'll get a divorce and then everything can go back to normal. I'll have my baby, and you'll have your freedom again.''

Jack frowned. ''Look, Beth, even if I were to agree to this crazy idea of yours—which I haven't done yet, you understand—then why go ahead with a sham marriage and an inevitable divorce? Why not keep it simple? Why not just crawl in the sack together and get the job done? Other couples do it that way?"

Beth gaped at him as if he should have already known the answer. Obviously he didn't know her as well as she thought. She drew in a deep breath and said, "Just because others do it that way doesn't make it right for me. Look, I'm not passing judgment on anyone else, but I can't just have an illegitimate child. It's not me."

"No, I guess you're right," he agreed. "But don't you see? It's not me, either. I happen to like being a bachelor. I don't want the responsibility of a wife and kid."

Beth felt a sudden pressure building within her. "I know that," she said quickly, "but that's what makes my plan so fantastic. I'll be the parent of this child, not you. You'll be…well, you'll be to him what you've always been to me. You'll be his best friend."

Folding his arms across his chest, Jack grew quiet and increasingly thoughtful over the following moments. Beth knew he was contemplating her words, and she wondered frantically what the outcome would be. Taking a deep breath, she held it and waited.

It was strange what occurred between two people when a little pressure was put on a long-standing relationship that had ages ago been taken for granted by both parties, she thought during Jack's silence. Scary, in fact. She had a lot to gain by what she was asking of Jack, but she also had a lot to lose, too, if she wasn't careful.

But she would be, she told herself. If he agreed to father her child, she would be very, very careful. Of that much she was certain.

"Look," she said, swallowing the umpteenth lump in her throat, "if you don't feel you can do this, I'll understand. Truly I will."

Giving a low, frustrated whistle, Jack ran his fingers through his hair. His gut was now boiling with an acid that was eating him alive. Beth was the one woman in the whole world who could turn him inside out like this.

He didn't particularly want the job of fathering a child for her, but then he didn't want anyone else to have it, either. Suddenly he couldn't stand the thought of her going to bed with some guy, just so she could get herself pregnant. Uh-uh. No way. He couldn't let something like that happen. Not to his Beth.

His real problem was, he'd never learned to refuse her anything. For better or for worse, he generally gave Beth what she wanted at some point. Why? Because it made him happy. But until today, she'd never before asked anything quite like this of him. Without question, this request was in a league all its own.

Drawing in a deep breath, Jack shook his head.

Of course, if he were going to be completely honest with himself, he was going to have to admit that the idea of sleeping with Beth wasn't all that foreign to him. She might be his best friend, but that didn't stop him from seeing her as a very attractive woman. He was, after all, a healthy male. Fortunately, though, he had always been able to keep his fantasies under control. Beth trusted him to be her best friend. He never, ever planned to betray that trust. Not for any reason.

Parenthood had always been her gig, not his. In fact, he didn't want the responsibility of being anyone's father. Not even to please Beth. So it was safe to say that if he did decide to go along with her idea—which he doubted he would—that she was right in thinking the child would be hers, not his. Of course, if he were to agree to her plan, he would always be there to lend a supporting hand when it came time for Beth to make all those tough parental decisions. He was her best friend, after all. She would need someone to lean on from time to time. And if she or the kid ever needed anything—anything at all—all they would have to do was ask.

Tossing Beth an anxious glance, he said, "Have you even thought of what will happen to us if I should decide to help you?"

Beth's heart began to pound. "What do you mean?"

"Us. You and me. We've been close friends a long time. How is that relationship going to be affected?"

She frowned. "Why should it be affected at all?"

He shrugged his shoulders. "I don't know. It just seems to me that it would be."

Beth gave him a smug look. "Well, it won't. The way I have it planned, we won't be married long enough for it to affect anything. I figure I'll be pregnant in two months, tops."

"Oh, really," he replied incredulously.

She could feel the adrenaline flowing through her veins as she sensed the rhythm of the moment changing in her favor. It made her feel flushed...excited. "I'm in good health. You're in good health. I feel quite certain that you'll have me pregnant in no time at all."

Stepping back in astonishment, Jack gave her a startled, though cocky grin. "Is that a fact?"

Beth beamed with renewed confidence. "That's right. Two months tops. I ought to be pregnant by then."

And what makes you so sure?"

She shrugged. "Just a feeling I have."

Jack searched her eyes for a long moment. "You've got this all figured out, haven't you?"

Every detail," she said proudly. "I knew it was imperative to our existing relationship that we set up the ground rules from day one."

Jack shook his head. "You and your damned rules, Beth. One of these days, those same rules are going to backfire on you."

She sucked in a hopeful breath. "Does that mean that you're thinking of helping me, Jack?"

He gave her a skeptical glance. "Do you really believe that this is the only way for you to get what you want?"

"Yes," she said, keeping a firm hold on the tidal wave of emotion suddenly raging through her body.

Using the tips of his fingers to rub his temples Jack

rocked back on his heels for what seemed like an endless moment. Finally, after releasing a heavy sigh, he said, "What the hell…I'm fighting a losing battle anyway. Besides, if it's what you need me to do…if you're sure it's what will make you happy in the long run, then what's a couple of months out of my life? You'd do the same for me."

"Oh, Jack," Beth said, biting back the flood of sudden tears. "Are you sure about this?"

"No…yes."

She gazed at him, her heart evident in her eyes.

"Yeah, I'm sure," he said at last, and in spite of a growing anticipation inside of him, he actually managed a grin.

"Oh, Jack, I don't know what to say. Thank you so much."

Beth couldn't contain her joy a moment longer. She threw her arms around his neck and planted a big, grateful kiss right on his mouth. It was just because she was so happy and wanted him to know it.

But all of a sudden, the kiss took a hundred-and-eighty-degree turn into something much more powerful than a mere thank-you peck on the lips. In fact, for one fleeting moment, Beth thought the ground was rocking beneath her feet.

Her mouth was covered by his.

He tasted like…well, like Jack. Just as she had always known he would. He tasted hot…and sexy, and the reality of what they were doing made her blood curdle. He opened his mouth and it seemed to her that he was beckoning for her to do the same.

This, she knew, was no longer just a simple little kiss between friends.

It was leading them somewhere—fast. Somewhere neither of them needed to go. Frankly it was going against every rule in her book. She had to end it now. She had no choice. Too much was at stake.

Immediately pulling away, Beth fought to regain her equilibrium. ''I—I don't know why I did that,'' she stammered.

Jack gave her a scorching glance that seemed to penetrate right through her.

Then without so much as a single word of warning, he groaned deep in his throat and jerked Beth back against his hard, solid frame in less than a heartbeat.

A second later his mouth came crashing down to claim hers.

This time, when the earth moved beneath her feet, Beth knew exactly what it was happening. But this time, instead of fighting it, she simply clung all the tighter to Jack and prayed that the moment didn't end too soon.

Because she knew without a doubt that she was going to hate herself when finally it did.

This was not part of her plan.

Nor could it ever be.

But since the moment was already out of her control, she saw no reason why she simply couldn't enjoy it while it lasted. Without a doubt, it was going to be the last time she ever let things go this far between herself and Jack.

For heaven's sake, he was her best friend. She felt almost guilty for enjoying his kiss.

It was just plain weird.

And yet unforgettably wonderful at the same time. Why else would she be pressing her body against his as though she wanted to become a part of him?

The weirdness she could handle.

But the part that was unforgettably wonderful—the part that was making her feel all hot inside—she could not.

She had to make sure this never happened between them again.

Chapter Three

Unfortunately Beth couldn't stop what was happening between herself and Jack, nor did a secret part of her really want to. And it was clear that Jack had no immediate plans to stop the kiss. She was trapped in the clutches of a sweet, agonizing hunger.

She moaned from the pressure of his lips on hers. It was the absolute craziest moment of her life. But what made it even crazier was the fact that, thus far, it was also her most thrilling.

But it was all a fluke. A faux pas, to be sure. Something that definitely shouldn't be happening.

Only it was.

Big time.

They were over the line, no doubt about it.

Someone needed to regain control of their outrageous behavior before it was too late.

It was probably already too late.

Jack deepened the kiss and again Beth moaned. Her response, as insignificant as it was to her, only seemed to ignite Jack's passions all the more. Keeping her pinned against him, he pushed his tongue into her mouth.

After the first shock waves of desire subsided, Beth began struggling to free herself.

She soon realized that her efforts in gaining her freedom were to no avail. Jack's hold on her was so much stronger than her puny effort, and she remained lodged in place against him.

She was on fire. This was getting really serious now. Someone had to do something—and quick.

Finally, Beth gave up, surrendering herself to the emotions surging through her body. Slipping her arms around Jack's neck, she did what she thought he wanted and opened her mouth to him.

And then, just like that, within the matter of another heartbeat, without the slightest warning of what was to come, he released her.

Startled, Beth stumbled back. ''Why did you kiss me like that?'' she asked.

Sucking in a deep breath, he shrugged. ''Look, you were the one who kissed me first. I just followed your lead.''

''But I didn't kiss you like that.''

His hands went to his hips. ''Well, you most certainly did.''

''W-well, I certainly didn't mean it,'' she stammered defensively. Frankly she'd never kissed a man like that in her whole life. Normally she was an old-fashioned prude when it came to such things—which was probably why she was, technically speaking, suffering from old-maid syndrome. But had she behaved prudently this time? Oh, no. This time she'd let herself go with all the abandon of a lovesick schoolgirl. And just how well was her good old friend Jack handling all of this? Like any typical man. He was trying to place all the blame on her.

Well, by golly, this wasn't her fault. Not entirely, anyway. She certainly hadn't forced him into kissing her. She had made her choices; he had made his. "Look, Jack," she said, "I was just trying to express my gratitude to you."

Without looking at her, Jack passed his hands through his hair. "Yeah, well, that's some kind of gratitude you have there, Beth," he said. "You ought to have it bottled as a lethal potion."

Beth's face burned with indignation, which came as a surprise to her, considering she was dealing with Jack. Ordinarily she would have had a laughable comeback for a remark like that from him. But for some reason she was completely speechless.

Looking down to smooth out the fabric of her straight black skirt, she said, "Look, I won't ever let something like that happen again."

"That's fine, Beth," he replied. "Only, there's one thing…"

She looked up. "Oh…?"

He gazed at her intently. "Frankly, I'd like to know who taught you how to kiss like that," he said.

Beth gaped at him. "What?"

"You heard me. That was some damned kiss. Where did you learn to do that?"

"I—I don't know what you mean," she said.

"Come on, Beth," he drawled in that deep, sexy voice of his. "Women like you don't generally kiss a man like that."

"Like *me?* Now what is that supposed to mean?" she asked indignantly.

"Take it from your old pal Jack," he said patronizingly, taking her by the shoulders and pulling her to him. "Women who have a strict moral code like you don't open their mouths like that when they kiss a man for the first time."

"Oh," Beth said. "Did I open my mouth?"

"Yeah," he said, a gleam coming to life in his eyes. "You sure did." He was still holding on to her shoulders. "Just tell me who the guy was who taught you to kiss like that? To tell you the truth, Beth, I never realized that you had gotten that serious with any of the guys you dated."

Beth frowned at him while trying desperately to make some sense of the moment. What was his problem anyway? No one had *taught* her to kiss like that. She had sensed that he wanted her to open her mouth, so she had.

Besides he had no right getting so personal with his line of questioning. They might be good friends and all, but enough was enough.

"I'm not going to answer that question, Jack. It's too personal even for you."

Suddenly it was Jack's turn to gape at her. His hands went slowly to his hips. "Is that a fact?" he said, narrowing his eyes as he studied her. "Well, for your information, I always thought we shared everything—even the personal stuff."

"Not everything, Jack," she said. "Some things are too private to share with anyone. There's always been certain topics that we've avoided between us."

He continued to stare at her openmouthed. "I was never aware of that. Would you mind giving me an example of what you mean?"

"Uh…yeah…well, of course," Beth said, pausing for a moment to gather her thoughts. "Okay, I've got one," she added quickly, suddenly gazing up at him with a surge of confidence. "Your little black book. The one you always carry with you. I've never questioned you about the names written inside." She shrugged. "I've always thought it was none of my business."

"My little black book…" he repeated in astonishment. "Jeez, Beth, I didn't know you had questions about it. What is it that you want to know?"

Unnerved by this whole line of questioning, Beth sighed heavily.

It wasn't that she hadn't ever wondered about all those women whose names she knew he had written down inside his address book. A secret part of her had always been curious about them. But she was smart enough to fill in the blanks. Besides, Jack had never been one to talk about the ups and downs of his love life. Unlike what she had always done with him. Of course, compared to his, her personal life had a "G" rating. Well, now it looked as though she was going to get her chance to see if she could handle the nitty-gritty details of his love life, after all. "Why do you always carry that address book with you?" she asked, keeping a close guard on her emotions.

Jack laughed, then held up his hands in surrender. "I don't anymore," he said. "And I haven't for a long time." He raised his arms above his head in a gesture of surrender. "Go ahead, check it out for yourself."

No way, Beth thought, but in spite of her best intentions to the contrary, her gaze automatically slid down the length of him, giving his lean-muscled body a thorough shakedown. It turned out to be a big mistake on her part. Giving Jackson Kincaid a shakedown of any degree was bound to cause a volatile reaction in any red-blooded woman—a reaction that even she, his best friend, wasn't immune to. Without warning, Beth's stomach bottomed out and that red blood of hers raced through her veins at record speed, causing her to feel hot and flushed all over. And to think Jack actually wanted her to frisk him. Well, he could forget that. For heaven's sake, if she touched him now her entire existence would suffer a meltdown.

Sliding her tongue over her bottom lip, she forced a smile. "Look, Jack, I don't need to check it out. If you say you're not carrying your little black book with you, then I believe you. Subject dropped."

Not for Jack, it wasn't. He ignored her reply and

instead stood with his feet spread apart, his shoulders back and his hands still placed behind his head. "No, go ahead," he said. "Frisk me. I want you to. I want you to see for yourself that I'm clean."

Frisk him indeed!

Her mouth grew as dry as powder.

"I don't need to frisk you, Jack. I believe you."

"I know. But I want you to frisk me anyway."

"I don't want to."

"Why not?" he asked, giving her a questioning look. But his hard, solid body remained poised for the shakedown he was expecting to get from her.

Beth's heart was pounding in her throat. "Why do I need a reason? Can't I just say I don't want to?"

"No," he replied. "If you don't have a reason, then you've got to frisk me, Beth. Those are the rules of this game."

"Who says there are rules?"

"I do," he replied.

Why wasn't she surprised, Beth wondered with a smirk.

Finally she rolled her eyes. How was she ever going to get herself out of this one? If she didn't do as he wanted, then she would have to give him a reason. And for the life of her, she couldn't come up with one good reason—other than the fact that she felt she was going to lose something of herself if she touched him in any way at that moment. But there was no way she could tell him that. After all the horsing around they had done over the years, he would think she was going nuts on him.

Damn Jack anyway, for putting her on the spot this way. She felt as though she was standing barefoot on hot, smoldering coals. Frankly, it felt as though Jack was the devil himself, smiling down at her. She wanted to run, but she didn't dare move a muscle.

Finally looking up, Beth found that the devil himself was still gazing down at her from his check-me-out position. "Well, what are you waiting for?" he asked.

For hell to freeze over, Beth thought. But obviously it wasn't going to happen now. Sighing heavily, she said, "Okay, Jack, you win."

He gave her a broad, sexy grin. One that would have completely shattered her composure if she hadn't been his best friend. It was at times like these that Beth was glad that she was oblivious to him in that way. It was probably the one factor she had going in her favor at the moment. Of course, her stomach sank to the floor, but that was nothing new. Certainly nothing to be concerned about.

Scantly breathing, she stepped up to Jack and began to lightly pat down the sides of his body, starting, of course, right under his armpits just as she'd seen the cops on television do. After all, if she was going to do this, she was going to do it right. By the book.

Her heart was pounding like mad. She felt breathless and couldn't believe what she was doing. More importantly, she couldn't believe what it was doing to her. This was Jack, for heaven's sake. Touching him had never been a problem for her before today. Something was incredibly wrong here.

It seemed that only a moment had passed, but already Beth had managed to inch her way down the outer part of Jack's firm body, all the way down to his shoes, in fact. Since this was a frisk down and she'd told herself that she was going to do it right, she paused only long enough to take a deep, steadying breath before placing her hand on the inseam of his jeans. Inch by inch she forced her fingers to crawl upward until she reached his midthighs. And then, just like that, as though the devil himself had placed a freeze on her, she stopped the whole process cold turkey.

Her hands began to tremble. She broke into a sweat. She thought the lump in her throat would surely close off her air passage, strangling her to a slow, agonizing death right there at his feet.

Okay, she told herself. This had gone far enough. Too far, in fact. Jack had pushed this gag to the limit, and they both knew it. Under no circumstances could she have brought herself to move her hand upward another centimeter, not even if she had been guaranteed all the money in the world.

Slowly Beth rose on wobbly legs, only to find the object of her immediate thoughts grinning down at her as if he knew what she was thinking.

It was just like Jack to thoroughly enjoy putting her in an awkward position like this. He often teased her about being old-fashioned and gladly took every opportunity that came along to help prove his point.

''See,'' he said a moment later, still grinning at her.

''It's like I told you. I don't have that little black book on me.''

In spite of her shaken condition, Beth managed to shrug. Because if Jack wasn't going to be rattled by all of this, then, by golly, she wasn't going to be, either. ''I couldn't care less,'' she said. ''It's Karen who thinks that it's some sort of a status symbol with you.''

Tilting his head back, Jack laughed out loud. ''And you believe her?''

''Well—no—I didn't say that,'' Beth replied indignantly.

''Then why did you frisk me?''

Beth gaped at him. ''Because you wanted me to.''

''It proved my point, didn't it?''

''Well…yes, but—''

He grinned. ''Now that we've got that settled, let's get back to the other thing.''

Beth frowned. ''What other thing?''

His grin broadened. ''The thing about where you learned to kiss with your mouth open. You never answered me when I asked you about it.''

''Oh, that other thing,'' Beth said begrudgingly. She shook her head. It was obvious that he wasn't going to leave the subject alone until she answered him.

''Okay, Jack,'' Beth said, ''since you seem to need an answer, I'll give you one. It just so happens that I never open my mouth when kissing a guy for the first time. True, I did on this one occasion, but only because I thought it was what you wanted me to do.

After all, if I can't trust *you* with a simple little kiss, then whom can I trust?''

''That was no simple little kiss,'' he said determinedly, heatedly.

Beth sighed heavily in defeat. ''Well, if it wasn't, then it was intended to be. Listen to me, Jack, I can't believe that we're going to let one little kiss get us all worked up like this. Frankly I thought we had the capacity as friends to rise above something like that.''

Jack glanced off at a distance for what seemed the longest time. Finally he turned back and gave her the slight resemblance of a smile. ''I can rise above it. I just don't know if I can forget it. But for our friendship I'll put it on the back burner.''

''That's a great idea,'' Beth replied in relief. ''Let's both put it on the back burner. We can always deal with it later.'' She knew that something had passed between them. Only, she didn't' know what. And, frankly, she didn't want to know.

''We're going to have to deal with it later,'' Jack said in that deep voice of his. ''Especially if you want to make that baby.''

Beth flushed. ''Oh…right.''

Eventually she and Jack got around to eating the meal she had prepared, and later, after they had decided that she would make arrangements for them to get married as soon as possible, Jack went home, promising to pick her up the next evening to attend Karen's party. Karen's get-together was going to be a good opportunity for them to tell all their friends what they were planning to do.

Beth went to bed that night feeling well-organized and in control of her life once more. Everything was going according to plan.

Her friendship with Jack was strong…solid…dependable. It could withstand anything.

Anything, she believed, but their falling in love.

Jack drove across town to his condo in the hopes that he would be able to fall into bed and go right to sleep. He was still suffering from jet lag due to his recent trip abroad. But at the moment he found himself suffering from a lot of other things, too. And they all had to do with Beth. For the time being, at least, he didn't want to think about it. Tomorrow he'd try to figure out just what kind of a mess he'd gotten himself into. For tonight, he just wanted to get some shut-eye.

But upon reaching his house and going straight to bed as he'd planned, he soon discovered that sleep was the farthest thing lurking in the corners of his mind.

Beth had really laid one on him this time. Never in a million years would he have ever suspected her of coming up with the idea of him being the father of her child.

But because he was her friend, because she meant so much to him, he knew that he was going to do whatever he could to see to it that she got what she wanted.

With that thought in mind, Jack rolled over in bed and tried once again to fall asleep. But when the sun rose in the east early the next day, he was still wide-awake to see its first peek on the dewy horizon.

Beth rose the next morning, her spirit renewed, her thoughts focused on the details of her upcoming marriage to Jack. She had to find a Justice of the Peace. Someone who would be willing to marry them on such short notice. And they needed to get a marriage license, too. And she would need some kind of a dress for the occasion. Suddenly there were so many details to take care of.

Eventually Beth got around to calling her secretary at the small real estate firm she owned and told her assistant that she was going to be late coming in that day. Caught up with the details of her wedding and then the impending sale of a house whose owners had just signed with her agency, Beth's entire morning whizzed by before she knew it. Her afternoon went by just as quickly and soon it was time to get ready for Karen's party.

At precisely six o'clock that evening, Jack drove up in front of her house in his '57 red-and-white Chevy convertible. Several years ago he had bought the car from an elderly man who wanted to get rid of it, and since then he and a friend had restored the vehicle to mint condition. He drove it occasionally, but only when the weather was spectacular and he could put the top down. Otherwise, he drove a four-wheel-drive sports wagon. But for summertime parties like the one they were going to tonight, Beth liked when he drove the vintage automobile.

She watched as Jack hopped out on the driver's side and strolled up her sidewalk, wearing jeans and a hunter green crew neck pullover shirt. His only flaw—and it wasn't even a flaw at all—was that when he appeared preoccupied with his thoughts, his eyebrows pulled down into a frown.

"Rough day at the office?" she asked as she joined him. They reached his car and she climbed in.

Jack snorted as he closed her door, then went around to his side. "You could say that. The president of the company has decided that we need to reorganize our sales campaign overseas."

"That sounds major," Beth replied.

Keeping his hands on the steering wheel, Jack tossed Beth a quick glance. "Let's just say this new ad campaign isn't something I'm looking forward to," he said. "Today, for instance, I was supposed to run an errand at noon, but I ended up being tied up in a meeting."

"Jack, you should've called me," Beth exclaimed. "I could've done the errand for you."

"Yeah, I know," he said. "But I already depend on you too much as it is."

He had never before minded depending on her to run his errands for him. Why now all of a sudden? she wondered. Unless...

Suddenly all the negative feelings she'd had concerning what she was asking him to do for her rose up, shaking her confidence. She could think of only one reason for the abrupt change in him. He was having second thoughts. Plain and simple. She had asked too much of him last night, and now he was trying to find a way to tell her.

Her and her big dreams of becoming a mother. What if she had ruined everything between them? What if she'd pushed him so far that he said he didn't want to be her friend any more? What was she going to do if that happened?

Hot, burning tears sprang to her eyes. Not wanting Jack to see them, she stared straight ahead and prayed the wind whipping across her face would blow them away. She should have known that asking him to be the father of her child was going too far. Any sane person would have realized that. But not her. Oh, no. She had to push things between them until they were way over the limit.

Shame on her, for ruining the best thing in her life.

They sat in silence the remainder of the trip.

When finally they reached their destination, Jack pulled his car into a parking spot at the curb in front of Karen's house, then killed the engine. "Hey," he said, placing his arm on the back of the seat and playfully squeezing her neck, "are you upset with me about something?" Grinning, he leaned forward and waited for her answer.

Without bothering to look his way, Beth glanced off in the distance. "Jack, why didn't you call me to run that errand for you today?"

"What?" he said quizzically, as though he didn't have the slightest notion what she was talking about. But he seemed to quickly recover. "Well, like I said,

I knew you were going to be busy. You'd said so yourself last night."

"I wasn't that busy," she countered.

He shrugged. "How was I to know that?"

"You would've known if you had called and asked me about it."

"Beth, what's with you?" he asked, giving her a frown. "Are you upset with me because I didn't call you today? Is that it? Is that what this is all about?"

Beth folded her arms at her waist. "Of course not. Besides, I'm not upset with you. I just think you should have called me to run that errand for you. Frankly I think you had a reason for not doing so."

Jack pulled his eyebrows back into a frown. "You know what I think?' he began. "I think this whole discussion isn't really about me at all. I think it's about you. I think you're having second thoughts about using me to father your baby, and you just don't know how to tell me."

Beth's mouth dropped open. "That's absurd," she said, her eyes growing round in disbelief. "Besides, I've already tried thinking of other possible candidates—believe me, I have—but I can't think of anyone else. Can you?"

Stunned, Jack was unprepared for answering a question like that. In fact, he was unprepared for any of this. He was just shooting his mouth off because Beth was acting so weird. But since she had seen fit to ask him such a question, he quickly decided that it might not be such a bad idea for him to try to find an answer to it and get them both off the hook. He wanted to be off the hook, didn't he?

Of course, he did. He hadn't asked for this job.

"Uh…how about that new guy?" he said offhandedly. But a moment later, he found his heart was pounding wildly as he waited anxiously for her reply. What if she thought someone he suggested could be a possible candidate? Then what?

Beth frowned. "What new guy?"

"You know, the one you just hired for your agency?"

"Allen Smith?" she asked, giving Jack an incredulous look.

"Yeah," Jack replied. "Him."

"Why would you think of him?"

He shrugged. "I don't know. I guess 'cause he's new in town."

"He's also married, Jack, with two kids," Beth said dryly.

"Oh, I didn't know. Well then, how about James?"

"James? James, who?"

"You know, the guy that just moved onto your street. He isn't married, is he?"

"I don't even know his last name."

"You could always find out," Jack replied.

Beth gave him a withering glare.

"Okay," he said noncommittally, "so you don't like any of my suggestions so far. Then how about George Stills? He seems like a nice enough fellow. And you've known him for years."

"He snores."

Immediately Jack came up straight in his seat and widened his eyes. "And just how do you know that?"

Beth smiled blandly. "I sold his girlfriend the Le-Blanc house on Oak Street last month and she just happened to mention that he snored."

Jack released a deep breath. Much to his astonishment, he found himself thoroughly relieved by that bit of information. Actually, he never thought he'd be so damned happy to hear that George Stills had himself a girlfriend—and that it wasn't Beth. "Okay, I give up," he said. "I guess you're right. You're stuck with me." But in that moment, he found himself damn happy that she was stuck with him. He just didn't see the importance of telling her how he felt. Knowing Beth as he did, she'd probably think that he was stepping over that line of hers—which, of course, he wasn't—and she'd put a stop to the whole thing.

Well, if anyone was going to be the father of her baby, it was going to be him. Because there was one thing he could always be sure of: She and her baby would be safe with him.

Just then a couple of their friends pulled up behind them at the curb and immediately approached his car. "Hey, are you two planning to sit in Jack's Chevy all night long?" one of them asked jokingly.

"We're coming," Jack answered. A moment later he opened Beth's car door and the two of them followed their friends toward the party already in progress.

Jack knew he didn't have a right to feel the way he did. But he couldn't help himself. He felt that Beth had been entrusted to his care a long time ago—since they were kids, in fact—and even today, it was a responsibility he took very seriously. Not that he actually ever said as much to anyone. It was just something inside of him. Something private. Something he took pride in.

"Guess what?" he said to her in a cocky manner just as they reached the gate leading into Karen's backyard.

"What?" Beth asked, looking up at him.

"You're in luck. *I* don't happen to snore."

"I know," she replied with a sassy little grin of her own.

Jack's gut knotted.

This obligation he felt toward Beth might not be turning out half bad after all. He hadn't even begun to let himself think much about the sex part of it yet.

But when he finally did, heaven help them both.

Chapter Four

After joining the party in Karen's backyard, Beth began searching the crowd for her friend. At some point, Jack stopped and joined in on a conversation with a couple of his buddies. Finally Beth spotted Karen's latest beau flipping burgers at the barbecue pit and hurried over to him. "Hi, Al. Where's Karen?" Beth asked.

"Beats me," he said over the sound of charring burgers as smoke bellowed up from the open pit. "Last time I saw her she was getting more ice for the drinks."

Beth smiled. "Okay. I'll find her." A moment later she spotted Karen at the food table, filling an empty bowl with potato chips.

"Hi, Karen," she said, walking up to her.

Karen whirled around. "Oh great, Beth, you're finally here. I've been waiting for you to show. What happened last night? How did things go with Jack?''

Beth beamed. "He's going to do it."

"So you talked him into it," Karen said. "I knew you would. Well, congratulations—not that I ever doubted for a moment how things would turn out," she replied laughingly.

"I still can't believe it's true," Beth answered, clapping her hands together. "Sometimes I think I need to pinch myself just to make sure that I'm not dreaming. I guess I'm paranoid, thinking he'll change his mind."

"He won't," Karen said flatly. "Not Jack. He knows that if he doesn't help you, some other guy will, and he isn't about to let that happen. Not if he can help it."

Beth chose to sidestep her friend's remark and said, "Since you were already having this party tonight, Jack and I decided it would be a good time to tell everyone what we have planned."

Karen shrugged. "Well…that isn't going to be necessary," she said.

"Why not?" Beth asked.

Karen didn't bother to look up from her task. "'Cause they already know."

"What do you mean?" Beth asked in astonishment. "How could they already know? I haven't told anyone yet—other than you."

"Look, they know, all right?"

"B-but how?"

"I told them."

Beth's mouth dropped opened. "You did what?" she exclaimed.

"Look, you and Jack were running late for the party and all that information was just sitting there on the end of my tongue. I blew it, okay. And I'm sorry. I should've kept your secret to myself until you got here, but I didn't. I told Melba and she spread the word around in nothing flat."

"Karen, how could you do such a thing?"

Karen shrugged. "Hey, look, I probably did you a favor. Now you don't have to stand there in front of everyone and try to explain yourself to them." She turned and walked around to the other side of the food table.

Beth followed right on her heels. "But what if Jack had said no to me."

Karen shrugged again. "I never thought of that. Besides, I knew he wouldn't. Look, I really am sorry. I know I should have kept my mouth shut and let you tell everyone. I wish I could take it all back, but I can't."

"I can't believe this," Beth said as she sank onto a nearby wooden stool and tried to get her thoughts together.

Karen came over to where she sat. "I know you're upset with me right now, and I really can't blame you for that. But do you want to know what most of our friends thought about your idea?"

That perked up Beth's attention. "Well…yes…of course, I do."

"Well…" Karen began, growing all seriouslike, "at first, everyone was somewhat stunned by the idea that you were going to marry Jack and then use him as some sort of a sperm donor for your baby. But then, the more I explained—and the more they thought about it—they began to remember how much you've always wanted a baby of your own. After a while, several of them were even saying that it seemed only natural for Jack to be the father." She shrugged. "Frankly I was impressed with their reactions. But then, everyone knows how close the two of you are."

Suddenly, at that precise moment, a major spill of some kind happened in the kitchen and Karen was called away to supervise the cleanup. Taking into consideration what her hastily departing friend had just told her, Beth rose from the stool in somewhat of a daze and went in search of Jack.

Making a sharp corner into Karen's house, she ran smack dab into a hard, solid frame. Instinctively she knew it was him. For whatever reason, he seemed to be in as big a hurry as she was.

"I've been looking for you," she said breathlessly.

"I've been looking for you, too," Jack said, his hands grabbing hold of her waist in an effort to steady them both. For a brief moment their eyes met and a surge of electricity passed between them.

Obviously stunned by it, Jack immediately dropped his hands from her waist and stepped back.

"Beth, everyone here at the party knows that we're planning to get married," he said.

"I know," Beth replied, gazing up at him.

"How did this happen?" he asked in amazement.

"It's my fault. I told Karen what I was planning to ask you when she came by my house yesterday afternoon. She decided to tell Melba, and Melba told everyone else—according to Karen anyway."

Jack smirked. "Do you know that someone I don't even know walked up to me a while ago and asked if it was true that I was going to be your sperm donor? And then she had the nerve to ask how you had come to choose me?"

Beth felt the blood drain from her face. "Oh, my goodness," she said, "it's gotten completely out of hand."

"Look," Jack said, "why don't we do ourselves a favor? Let's get out of here in one piece while we still can. We can always call our friends tomorrow and tell them what we want them to know."

As far as Beth was concerned, that was the best idea she'd heard all night. "I'm game. What do you have in mind?"

He glanced up at the nighttime sky. "Well, since it's such a nice evening, how about a drive in the country?" he asked.

"Oh, Jack," Beth said, her face flushing with excitement, "that sounds like a wonderful idea."

He grinned. "I thought you might like it."

"I'll get my purse."

"And I'll wait for you by the side gate. We'll make our escape from there," he answered.

"I have to find Karen first," Beth said, "and explain that we're leaving."

"Leave that to me. Just get your purse so we can get out of here."

She smiled knowingly. "I'll be back in a minute."

Beth hurried off to get her purse from inside the house. A minute later she met up with Jack at the side gate. "Did you find Karen?"

"Yeah."

"Was she upset about our leaving the party?"

"She didn't seem to be. I think she understood."

"Jack…since we're planning to drive out to the country anyway, could we please go by Wilibee's pond? I haven't been out there in years."

Wilibee's pond, Jack thought with a sudden, unexpected jolt to his system. It had been years, it seemed, since he had last thought about that place. It had been even more years since he and Beth had been out there together.

Wilibee's pond. One of his most memorable occasions at the small, sandy-bottomed, fresh water pond had been when old man Wilibee caught him and Beth skinny-dipping together. How old had they been anyway? Ten? Eleven? He couldn't remember anymore. All he could recall was that they had ridden their bikes out there one hot July afternoon and the idea of swimming naked had just evolved from their wanting to get cooled off from the heat. Beth, of course, hadn't wanted to ruin her clothes because she knew her mother was strict about such things. They were just kids at the time and getting naked hadn't seemed like such a big deal to them anyway. So they had simply removed all their clothes and dove into the cool water. It wasn't long after when old man Wilibee had shown up in a tirade, saying that he'd just called their parents to tattle on what they were up to.

His parents had arrived on the scene first and gave him a good tongue-lashing—not to mention a list of warnings of what was going to happen to him if he ever decided to do something so stupid again. But when Beth's parents arrived, they had gone completely bonkers over the incident and had punished her for two whole months. Not only that, but they had gone out of their way to see to it that she had felt humiliated by what she'd been caught doing. The fact that they had been just kids at the time seemed of no consequence to her parents or to old man Wilibee. Soon afterward Beth's parents had split up for good and he remembered now how the whole episode, including her parents' breakup, had been pretty tough on her. She had changed after that incident, and for a long time she had kept even him at arm's length. He hadn't blamed her, though. He probably would have done the same thing if something similar had happened to him.

Wilibee's pond. It held a lot of old memories for them—some good, some bad—although, he thought that even Beth would have agreed most of them were good. In any case, it was the perfect setting for what he had in mind for them for the rest of the night.

Without a doubt, he liked the idea that he and Beth were going to have the rest of the night all to themselves. That was how he liked it anyway…when it was just him and her, sitting somewhere—anywhere—together, side by side, with all their hopes and dreams tucked in all around them.

Yeah, that was how he liked it, all right. Just him and Beth and that comfortable, satisfied feeling of knowing he was her best friend in the whole wide world, and that when she needed anything—even a father for the child she wanted to have so badly—he was the one she turned to.

Once they were settled again in his Chevy, Jack headed out of town, their hair blowing wildly in the warm, nighttime breeze. The moon was so full and bright that it's light overshadowed the stars, and it was only every now and then that one could be seen twinkling above.

Eventually Jack turned his car off the main highway and headed down a narrow lane through a small patch of woods until he reached a clearing. Glistening in the moonlight as though waiting for their return was Wilibee's pond, just as they remembered it.

''Oh, Jack, it's the same,'' Beth said, a lump forming in her throat.

"Yeah, it is," Jack replied in awe. A second later, he opened his car door and got out. Turning back to look at Beth, he said, "Come on, what are you waiting for? Let's check out the water."

"The water...?" she said, dumbfounded. "Jack, surely you're not thinking of—"

But her words died on her lips because Jack was already way ahead of her and apparently not listening to a thing she said.

She opened her car door and got out, trying her best to catch up with him. Finally she gave up and just followed at her own pace. She was glad that she had thought of coming here. The feel...the smell...was just like old times.

Well, almost.

Some things had changed.

For instance, she and Jack were no longer kids.

"Look over there," he said, pointing toward a tall tree on the edge of the bank halfway around the other side of the pond. "Remember the old vine we used to swing on? I wonder if it's still there."

"Surely not," Beth replied, watching him hurry toward the tree to check it out for himself. Lucky for them, there was enough moonlight that they could see where they were going.

Before Beth could gather her wits and follow him, Jack was already at the tree, tugging on something that resembled a vine. Of course, it was questionable whether or not what he'd found was actually the vine they had used as kids. For heaven's sake, that had been twenty-some-odd years ago. But she wasn't going to be the one to tell him that. He seemed to be having too much fun thinking that the vine they had used and the one he had just found were one and the same. Who knew, maybe they were.

Beth cupped her hands around her mouth. "You're going to get all dirty," she warned from where she stood.

Jack stopped tugging on the vine and turned his attention to the tree itself. He began to examine it closely.

"What are you looking for?" she yelled.

He didn't answer her for several moments. Then, suddenly, he turned and began motioning with his hand for her to join him. "Come over here, Beth, and see this," he shouted.

"What is it?" she asked.

Again, he motioned with his hand. "Come here."

It was obvious that he wasn't going to tell her what he'd found. Apparently he wanted her to see it for herself.

Taking a deep breath, Beth began strolling along the pond's outer bank, all the while watching her step as she headed in Jack's direction. But within seconds it was apparent that her casual stroll wasn't getting her there quick enough for him. Hurrying in her direction, he met her halfway. "Close your eyes," he said the moment he was near enough.

"What?"

"Just do as I say and close your eyes," he said.

She shrugged nonchalantly and then closed her eyes. "This had better be good, Jack."

"It will be," he said, taking her by the hands and leading her in the direction he had come from. "Now just follow me."

"I'm trying," she said rather dryly. "But I could do a better job of it if you just slowed down."

"Just don't peek," he replied.

Who was he trying to kid? she wondered. As if she had time to worry about peeking. She was just trying to stay on her feet, for heaven's sake. "You're going too fast," she cried out.

Finally he slowed down.

"Thank you," she said with a hint of sarcasm.

"Okay, you can open your eyes now," he said a few moments later.

Beth's eyes fluttered open, but all she saw was the trunk of the tree Jack had been examining. Finally, though, her eyes focused on what she thought he was talking about.

"Do you remember when we did this?" he asked, pointing to a particular area of the trunk. He brushed his fingers along a faint carving. It read, *Jack & Beth*.

Her heart began to pound. Of course, she remembered.

Placing his hands on his hips, Jack turned to study the water. "You know what I think?" he said. "I think we ought to go in for a swim."

Beth's heart skipped a beat and she laughed nervously. "Not me."

He turned and grinned at her. "Why not? The water looks great. I bet it's cool."

She folded her arms across her chest. "It doesn't matter to me what the water temperature is. I'm not getting in. Not this time."

"Give me one good reason why not."

"There's a million reasons why not—all of which start with the fact that I don't have a swimsuit with me."

"Who needs a swimsuit?"

Somehow she had known he was going to say that.

As if her lack of an answer in that moment was all the answer he needed, Jack began to unfasten the buckle of his belt.

"What are you doing?" Beth asked, horrified to see him going ahead with his plan in spite of her objections.

"I'm taking off my clothes," he said matter-of-factly. "Come on, Beth. Be a sport. Jump in with me."

Jump in, indeed. Not in her wildest dreams would she do something like that…again. The one and only time she had decided to strip naked with a male had been to go swimming with Jack in this very pond when she was ten years old and it had turned out to be disastrous. Yeah, sure, times had changed. She was all grown up now, and so was Jack. But who was to say that getting naked with him this time wouldn't be another catastrophe? In fact, in one way or another, she was almost certain that it would be.

All of a sudden, in one quick move, Jack pulled his shirt off from over his head and tossed it to the ground.

Beth's breath locked in her throat. She gaped at him, at the ease in which he felt comfortable stripping off his clothes right there in front of her. Not that she hadn't seen him bare-chested before. She'd seen him that way more times than she could remember. But suddenly it was as though she was *really* seeing him for the first time. His skin glistened in the moonlight. Worse, the deep shadows that fell around them only made his partial nakedness seem all the more alluring...all the more dangerous...all the more sexy. Swallowing hard, she scanned down his body, paying close attention to the lean muscles in his chest and abdomen. A sparse patch of light brown curly hair covered the center of his chest. In that moment she could have tried to deny it all she wanted, but there was a definite part of her that liked what she was seeing. Liked it a lot, in fact.

She felt almost dizzy, trying to make a decision about what she should do. With all the pulse points on her body throbbing to an all-time high, she dragged her eyes away from Jack and glanced out over Wilibee's pond in an effort to gather her thoughts. Surprisingly she found that she very much wanted to get naked and go skinny-dipping with him.

For old times' sake, of course.

Or perhaps to prove a point. An old point.

Of course, that was it in a nutshell.

She hadn't done anything wrong all those years ago when she had gone skinny-dipping with him, and she was ready now to prove it to herself. And to Jack. And to the whole world, if necessary.

Or was she?

Of course, she was.

Suddenly making up her mind faster than she would have ever dreamed possible of herself, Beth brought her hands to the button at the top of her blouse and began to unfasten it.

She glanced up at Jack and saw he had stopped in his own efforts to get undressed. He was grinning at her.

A second later, she grinned, too.

Chapter Five

Not wanting to disrupt the momentum that held her spellbound for fear of losing her courage, Beth breathed in as little oxygen as possible while working her fingers down the front of her silk blouse, unfastening one button at a time. Jack stood watching her, a slight grin still lingering at the corners of his mouth. With every moment that slipped by Beth knew she was pushing herself closer and closer to the point of no return. If there was ever a chance of reconsidering her actions, it was now. Five minutes down the road was going to be too late.

But since her mind was already made up, Beth continued to unfasten the buttons of her blouse.

After fumbling with her last one, she lifted her gaze to meet Jack's and smiled. A moment later, she slipped her blouse off her shoulders and let it fall to the ground behind her.

She heard Jack suck in his breath. The grin that had lingered for so long on his face suddenly vanished.

"Look at you," he said reverently, his eyes burning with an intensity she'd never seen in them before.

Suddenly brave beyond anything she could have imagined for herself, Beth reached out and ran the tips of her fingers down the center of his chest, feeling the different textures of his body, his skin…the hard muscles that rippled over his rib cage. She was on fire. "Look at you," she said in a throaty voice.

Using the backs of his hands, Jack pushed her long hair behind her shoulders. Then he drifted his touch lightly down her shoulders and arms, causing a cascade of chills to rake over her body and causing her bra straps to fall.

"We shouldn't be doing this, Jack. We both know it's dangerous."

"Then what should we be doing?" he asked, his eyes glistening, his voice velvety smooth. In that moment she knew that even if she were to have an answer for him, he wasn't planning to pay attention.

Surprisingly she didn't want to pay attention, either, but they had to. Her plan depended on it. It was a matter of rules and principles—and just plain survival.

"Let's just put our clothes back on," Beth said, dropping her gaze to the ground in order to find her blouse.

But Jack immediately grabbed her by the shoulders

and forced her attention back to him. "Not yet, Beth," he said.

Their eyes met and held. A chill passed down her body. "I'm scared, Jack," she said, trembling in spite of herself.

"Don't be scared," he replied. "I'd never hurt you. Not in a million years."

"No, you don't understand. This kind of behavior could ruin our friendship."

"Don't be scared of that. I have everything under control. And so do you. We're okay."

He might be okay. But she sure wasn't. So why didn't she just stop this madness…this…this insanity?

"Show me the rest of your body," he said in that rich drawl of his. "I've waited a long time to see you like this."

"Since before puberty, I bet," Beth said jokingly, trying to make light of the moment.

But he didn't laugh.

This was getting serious. Too serious, in fact. She didn't even know how to stop it anymore. Nor did she really want to, she realized. It was exciting… fun…sexy.

And she had Jack's reassurance that they were okay. They weren't over the limit—yet. And he'd never steered her wrong before. Therefore, she saw no reason why she shouldn't trust him now. After all, he was her closest, dearest friend in the whole world. If she couldn't trust him, whom could she trust?

Jack leaned forward and gave her a feather-light

kiss on the mouth, then pulled away and smiled. Using his index finger, he traced the French cut of her bra, making Beth distinctly aware that the skimpy mauve satin undergarment she wore was very provocative, to say the least. Especially from a male's point of view, she supposed. If only she had known that she would be undressing in front of him tonight, she would have worn something less revealing. Something more matronly. Something that wasn't pushing her boobs out like two cypress knees poking out of the backwaters of south Louisiana. But, of course, she had had no warning…no sign that she was going to strip down naked tonight in front of her best friend. This was all spur-of-the-moment. No doubt, tomorrow she would hate herself for it.

Dazed from all the indecisions consuming her thoughts, Beth followed Jack's movement as he reached just beneath her cleavage and in one easy, fluid motion unfastened the front clasp of her bra. Suddenly she was naked from the waist up. Thank goodness it was hot outdoors and not freezing cold. As it was, her nipples hardened.

Good grief, she could hardly breathe. She thought she would die from the sheer titillation of it all.

"Beth," Jack said, his voice hoarse…hesitant. A moment later he began rubbing the back of his thumb against the fullness of her left breast, eventually running the tips of all his fingers tantalizingly slow over the mound, the nipple, and then on down her rib cage toward her waistline. Hooking one finger in a belt loop on her jeans, he pulled her closer to him. "I never knew you were so beautiful," he said.

Beth was trembling, but she had never in her life felt more beautiful than she did in that moment. His heated gaze warmed her flesh, making her skin flush with excitement. She heard the air rush from Jack's lungs and knew he was struggling with his emotions, too. But, heaven help her, she didn't want him to stop touching her. Not now. Not ever.

But it was the excitement she was caught up in, she told herself. Of that much she was certain. It had nothing whatsoever to do with desire. And now that she had made the distinction, she was ready to continue with the moment.

Pulling her roughly against him, Jack began kissing her, first at the base of her neck, then right below her ear. Finally, just a second before she thought she would die if he didn't continue, he took her lips with a sense of urgency that left her breathless.

Her arms went around his neck. Groaning, he pushed his tongue into her mouth, and it seemed to Beth that in that moment hot liquid poured from everywhere inside her. Hot, potent liquid that had her burning up. She thrust her body against his.

And then they heard something—a vehicle, perhaps—and immediately sprang apart. Sure enough, it was a deputy sheriff's patrol car, and its blue light was flashing. It seemed they were in deep trouble now, Beth thought. And not like the first time, when it had been just old man Wilibee who came storming in on them. With her luck, this time could end up being front page news.

After gathering her wits, she scrambled for her blouse, but it was Jack who found it and helped her slip it back on over her shoulders. Then he quickly pulled his shirt over his head.

The officer drove the patrol car closer. Finally he turned off the flashing blue light and rolled down his window three-quarters of the way. He had a large flashlight, which he shined right on Jack's face. "Hey, buddy, didn't you see the signs when you turned off the main highway? This is posted land nowadays—new owners and all. There's no trespassing allowed."

Jack held out his hands. "To tell you the truth, Officer, I didn't notice anything. We used to come here when we were kids and just decided to come back tonight on a whim. Sorry. We didn't mean to break any laws."

"Well…" the cop began, flashing his light only briefly at Beth, "I can't see where there's been any harm done. Just be on your way."

"Sure enough, Officer," Jack replied.

The deputy rolled his window back up, turned his patrol car around and a few moments later drove back down the lane toward the highway.

Beth's nerves were shot. In fact, they were double shot.

It wasn't enough that she had just thrown herself at Jack, practically begging her best friend to seduce her with her lurid behavior, but she had just been stopped from making the biggest mistake of her life by a police officer, no less. For heaven's sake, what had she been thinking of?

Well, she knew one thing. She and Jack had to get out of here—and fast. And not just because the police officer had said so. There were other reasons, just as crucial to their survival.

She had her blouse all buttoned up and was ready to go when Jack grabbed hold of her wrists, stopping her hurried efforts to get composed. "Slow down, Beth. The cop's gone. And it isn't likely he'll be coming back anytime soon. We've got plenty of time to get ourselves dressed and out of here."

But Beth was so wound up that she didn't really hear a word he said. She pulled herself free and headed for the car. "Let's go, Jack. Hurry up."

"Beth, wait," he countered.

She turned back to face him.

"Aren't you forgetting something?" he inquired pointedly.

Beth frowned.

He bent over and picked up that "something" he was talking about from the ground. *Oops, her bra.* "Aren't you forgetting this?" he asked.

With a deepening frown on her face to match the aggravation she now felt toward herself, Beth marched back to where he stood and tried taking her piece of clothing away from him.

"Uh-uh," he said. "I took this bra off of you. I'm putting it back on."

In his wildest dreams, Beth thought. No one was

putting that bra back on her tonight. It wasn't necessary anyway. She already had her blouse on. "You're bringing me straight home, Jack, so there's no need to worry about it now."

"Oh, but I insist on worrying about it now, Beth," he said. "If I don't, then who will? You seem to care less. Besides, I'm the party responsible for taking it off. The least you can do is let me rectify that."

He began unfastening the buttons to her blouse. *The very buttons she had just fastened.*

"Now wait a minute, Jack," she said, trying to stop him.

But he brushed her hands away. "Behave, Beth. This won't take me but a moment," he said.

Behave, indeed.

She glared at him, trying to decide whether or not she wanted to continue arguing her point.

But before she could even make that decision, she found herself naked again from the waist up. It happened that fast. He was really getting good at taking her clothes off.

Too good, in fact.

"You really are beautiful, Beth," he said, his gaze poring over her in a gentle, caring way.

Her breath locked in her throat. Funny thing was, she felt all tingly and beautiful inside, just as he said.

Suddenly a combination of emotions sprang up in her from out of nowhere, allowing an enormous fear to seize hold of her heart. A huge, diehard fear that warned her against letting the situation between them get any more out of hand. She couldn't let that happen. Not again. Not so soon. Not ever.

Her thoughts must have shown on her face, because Jack abruptly reined in his actions. A moment later he helped her slip her arms through the straps of her bra and then secured the undergarment in place without further ado. "There. See, I told you," he said. "I can touch you and still be your best friend."

Beth breathed a sigh of relief. "Just don't do something crazy like fall in love with me, Jack. That would ruin everything."

"Me?" he said, shaking his head as if that was the most unheard of possibility in all the world. "Fall in love with you? No way, José."

Then he cleared his throat. "Just don't you go and fall in love with me," he added, fastening the last of the buttons on her blouse. He straightened her collar and smiled at her in that way she knew and loved. It was such a relief to have her old friend Jack back.

"You needn't worry about that," Beth replied. "I'm not that dumb."

"See," he said, giving her the sexiest grin she'd ever seen. "I told you that we were okay. You've got to learn to trust me, Beth."

"Oh, but I do trust you, Jack. I trust you with my life."

He bent over and kissed the tip of her nose. "Then let's get out of here before that cop decides to come back and see if we've obeyed the law."

Moments later they were back in Jack's Chevy, heading into town, and the whole episode of their kissing and touching, of their wanting, was behind them.

They had just made it over another hurdle in their relationship. And according to what Jack said, they had come out smelling like roses.

When Beth fell into bed that night, she couldn't have been more pleased.

Her plan was going to work.

The ringing of a telephone awakened Beth in the dead of night. It seemed she'd just closed her eyes to go to sleep. She couldn't imagine who was calling her at this late hour, unless her two divorced parents were at it again and one of them was calling her to whine about the other. That happened every so often, like clockwork.

"Hello," she said, her voice more of a croak.

"Beth…?"

She cleared her throat. "Yes."

"Now that sounds more like you," he said, laughingly.

"Jack…Jack, is that you?" Beth forced herself to wake up and propped herself up on one elbow.

"Yeah," he said with a chuckle. "Who else other than your parents would call you at three o'clock in the morning just to talk?"

"You want to talk?"

"Uh-huh."

She yawned first and then said, "About what, for heaven's sake?"

"About anything. I can't sleep. I thought you'd keep me company for a while."

She groaned. "What can we possibly talk about at this time of morning?"

"We can talk about anything," he said, as though he was halfway expecting her to have a topic of discussion right there on the tip of her tongue. Her brain wasn't even awake yet.

When it was obvious she had nothing in mind to say, he whispered, "Beth, do you ever sleep nude?"

Beth rolled over flat on her back and at first laughed out loud. "Now why in heaven's name would you want to know something like that?"

"Hey," he said, "I'm just trying to make conversation."

"No. I never sleep nude."

"But you would be, wouldn't you, if you had a lover with you?"

Suddenly it felt as though her lungs were decompressing and she couldn't breathe. This line of questioning wasn't exactly what she had been expecting from him, especially not during a phone conversation at three o'clock in the morning.

"Jack, are you all right?"

"Not really," he said. "I can't seem to forget what happened between us at Wilibee's pond. I can't close my eyes without seeing how beautiful you were right before that deputy showed up. I haven't slept a wink all night."

This time, Beth's lungs really did decompress. Somehow, in the back of her mind, she'd known all along that his phone call had something to do with what happened at Wilibee's pond.

"What happened between us at Wilibee's pond was a mistake, Jack. We both know that. I'm just thankful that the deputy sheriff came along when he did."

"Yeah, well, if it's that simple for you to put aside, then come over here and try telling that to my libido."

"Just don't think about it," she said, trying to keep a tight rein on her own emotions.

"Come on, Beth, it isn't that simple, and you know it."

Did she? Beth wondered. Of course, she did. She'd had her own problems trying to fall asleep tonight because of the intensity of what had happened between them at the pond. She drew in a deep breath. "Okay, Jack, so it isn't that simple. But that's the way it has to be…for now. We can deal with these feelings when—"

"When we try to make a baby," he said softly, seductively. There was a momentary pause. Finally he groaned, "You're not helping me out at all with this."

"I'm doing the best I can," she said with a sigh. It was obvious to Beth that Jack had no idea how difficult this was for her. She had feelings, too. Feelings she didn't want to examine too closely at the moment. She had enough on her mind as it was.

"Jack," she said, "I think the best thing I can do

for now is hang up before this conversation goes any further. Try and get some sleep, okay? Good night.''

''Beth, wait!'' he exclaimed. ''Look, there is something else I want to talk to you about.''

''Not tonight, Jack.''

''It won't take but a second.''

She sighed heavily into the receiver so that he would think her patience was wearing thin. And, in fact, it was.

But she stayed on the line anyway, and waited to hear what he had to say.

''A colleague of mine is coming into town tomorrow for a couple of days of meetings at the office,'' he said after a moment. ''Anyway, my boss asked me to take him to dinner tomorrow night, and I thought you might like to join us. Malone has been wanting to meet you for some time now. What do you say? Can you come?''

''Why does he want to meet me, for heaven's sake?''

''I guess 'cause I talk about you a lot.''

''Oh.''

''Will you come?''

''Well, I guess so. If you want me to,'' she replied.

''Great. Then I'll call you tomorrow with the details. Oh—and, Beth. Take my advice. Try sleeping in the nude now and then. After all, you'll have to soon enough.''

Then he hung up the phone.

When Beth woke up the next morning, she was mildly surprised to find herself naked in bed. Smiling to herself, she remembered that after hanging up with Jack last night—or, rather, this morning—she had decided on a whim to take his advice about sleeping naked. Now, after running her hands slowly down the sides of her body to feel the texture of her own skin, she stretched her arms over her head and yawned widely. She certainly had slept sound. She felt rested and ready for the day.

After climbing out of bed, she got ready for work and was the first one at her realty office that morning. By the time the others arrived and the workday began full force, she had already taken care of several details concerning her and Jack's upcoming marriage. She had found a Justice of the Peace to marry them on Saturday, and she had decided that the off-white silk suit she already had hanging in her closet was going to be perfect for the occasion. She'd only worn it once, to Jack's cousins's baby's baptismal ceremony last year. There was absolutely no reason for her not to consider wearing it again, this time to her own wedding. Her hair…well, she still didn't know exactly what she was going to do with it. But surely she or Karen would come up with an idea between now and Saturday. In the meantime, she had also decided that she and Jack would have cake and champagne for after their ceremony. Something had to be traditional about her wedding, after all. In any case, she had an appointment with a baker that very evening to see what he had to offer.

Beth broke the news about her upcoming wedding to her employees later that morning in the coffee room. She didn't give them all the details, just the necessary ones. After last night, she'd learned her lesson about giving out too much information concerning her private life. As it was, three of her friends who'd attended Karen's party the night before, as well as Karen herself—who, by the way, knew all the details already—had called her at work this morning, wanting to know what exactly was going on between her and Jack. She kept having to repeat the same old story, over and over again.

Blessedly, Beth had appointments most of the day that kept her out of the office, but when she finally checked in at five o'clock, there was a message on her desk from Jack, saying he would pick her up around seven for dinner with his colleague.

Darn, Beth thought. She had forgotten that she agreed to the dinner. Now what? She had that appointment with the baker tonight at six-thirty. She supposed that she had enough time to make both dates, if she tried. Besides, Jack had mentioned the name of the restaurant where they would be dining. She could always join them there after she finished placing her order with the baker.

She checked her wristwatch. It was already after five. She called Jack's office, but the answering service picked up. She didn't bother leaving a message. Instead she called his home and left a brief one on his answering machine, telling him what she was planning to do. Then she rushed home, took a quick shower, did her hair up off her shoulders and slipped into one of her nicer cocktail dresses. It was black,

straight and low-cut down the back—perfect, she
thought, for tonight's restaurant with its low lighting,
plush carpeting and fine china dining. Lobster and
Steak "à la Vinet" were the chef's specialties, and
the piano bar located in the restaurant was one of the
best places around for a quiet, romantic evening.
Since she was meeting the baker first, she was going
to have to explain to him why she was dressed as she
was. She felt certain he would understand.

As it turned out, he did—and so did his wife and
four children. By the time that he and Beth—and his
wife and four children—had decided on the cake she
wanted for her wedding, it was already past seven-
fifteen. Racing from the bakery, she got into her car
and hurried downtown to the restaurant to meet with
Jack and his colleague. She only hoped that her late-
ness hadn't stopped them from going ahead with their
evening as planned.

But when Beth pulled into the restaurant's parking
lot, she didn't see Jack's car in any of the designated
places. Of course, she didn't exactly go around the
whole lot, looking for his car. She just thought she
would have seen it as she pulled in. Only she hadn't.

She went inside.

After approaching the hostess, she gave the young
woman Jack's name, then gazed out over the dining
room for herself, thinking she would see him. She
didn't.

"Your table is for a party of three," the hostess
said.

"That's right," Beth answered, smiling.

"You're the second of your party to arrive. There's a gentleman already seated. I'll bring you to your table now, ma'am," the hostess politely said.

Beth immediately assumed that the gentleman who was already seated at their table was Jack, and she found herself wondering fleetingly if his colleague was still planning to join them.

"This way, ma'am."

Beth followed the hostess to where she thought she would find Jack. But instead, a dark-haired, incredibly handsome man in a dark three-piece business suit was sitting at the table.

"There must be some mistake," Beth said hesitantly.

The gentleman quickly stood. "Ahh...you must be Beth," he began. "I'm Franko Malone, Jack's colleague." He practically snapped to attention right in front of her. Beth could only watch as he did. "I'm honored to meet you at last," he said, taking her hand and placing a kiss right above her knuckles. "Jack speaks so highly of you."

"He does?" Beth said, awed down to her toes that this...this gorgeous man actually knew who she was. Franko. For heaven's sake, what a hunk of a name for a hunk of a guy. "P-pleased to meet you," she finally stammered.

He was still holding her hand. "The pleasure is all mine, I assure you." Then he let go of her and pulled out the chair next to him. "Have a seat, my dear, and let us wait for our good friend Jack to arrive."

She sat, although truthfully it felt as if she was

sitting on air, not a chair. Franko Malone was so much more than she had been expecting, and she wondered momentarily if her clear red lipstick was still on and looking as dewy as the labeling on its package said it would after hours of wear.

Finally she pulled herself together enough to ask, "Where is Jack? Shouldn't he be here already?"

"Jack…?" he said, as though the name were completely foreign to him. Actually Beth was thinking that maybe he was foreign. He had an accent of some kind.

"Ah, Jack, yes…" he finally got around to saying. "Well, he told me that he had something he had to do first and that he might be running late. But don't you fret, my dear Beth," he said, smiling at her, "I promise to do everything within my power to keep you entertained until our boy Jack shows up."

Beth frowned fleetingly. It wasn't like Jack to be late. But obviously he would be tonight. She smiled back at Franko.

"I've taken the liberty of ordering a bottle of wine for our table. Would you care for a glass?" he asked.

Such manners. No doubt about it, this guy could easily swoop her off her feet. My, my, what even white teeth he had. *Didn't that line come from a nursery rhyme somewhere?* And he was so meticulously dressed, too. Not a hair out of place. She was impressed with him.

"Yes, thank you," she said. "I'd like that very much."

He took her glass and poured a couple of ounces

of wine in it. "Let's make a toast," he said smoothly. They raised their glasses. "To Jack, for finally introducing me to his gorgeous friend Beth."

Beth glowed with pleasure from hearing him praise her. But she was also a little embarrassed by it, too. She had just met the guy, but he certainly didn't mind coming on a little strong. Frankly the intensity in his gaze was beginning to make her feel somewhat uneasy.

"To Jack," she said. "The best friend a girl could ever have."

They took sips from their wineglasses and then placed them down on the table. "I'm glad Jack is your friend," Franko said a moment later, leaning in close to her. "He can be your friend. I'd rather be something else, if you know what I mean."

Good grief, did she ever, Beth thought to herself, almost choking on her wine. She coughed twice, and then her stomach knotted. She should have known that a guy as good-looking as Franko was too good to be true. When it came to Knights in Shining Armor, that was usually how it went for her.

She frowned. Where was Jack when she needed him anyway?

He should have been here by now.

And when he got here, she was going to drag him off to the side and tell him what she thought of him leaving her alone like this to entertain *his* colleague. The guy was charming…and good-looking…but—

But it wasn't enough.

Boy, was she going to give Jack a piece of her mind just as soon as he got here.

"Would you like to dance?" Franko asked.

Just her luck, Beth thought to herself. Prince Charming at last. And what did she think of him? Frankly she wasn't all that sure. He was handsome, yes, and nice—but he wasn't Jack. And there was a certain something about him that was beginning to bother her a lot. He gave her the feeling that he thought he already knew her far better than she knew herself, and she didn't like it one bit. One thing for sure: She could never trust him, not like she did Jack.

But, because Jack had asked her to join him and his colleague for dinner tonight, she had enough grit in her to sit here with a smile on her face and bear this man's company for one short evening. If the shoe had been on the other foot, Jack would have done the same for her.

Without a doubt.

Darn it.

Where was he anyway?

Chapter Six

Beth glanced at Franko and smiled. But from the over-confident look in his eyes, she had the feeling that a dance with him was going to be a mistake. Since he already seemed to know so much about her—thanks, no less, to her good friend Jack—he probably knew that she loved to dance. How could she possibly refuse him without giving him a valid excuse? And, at the moment, she couldn't think of a single one. After taking a deep breath, she offered him her hand. ''I suppose one dance won't hurt anything,'' she said.

He smiled. The next thing she knew, they were on the dance floor.

And just as she had feared, what should have been a simple waltz turned out to be a tug-of-war. But not because she was having trouble keeping up with

Franko's footsteps. She had no problem with that. She just couldn't seem to keep up with his hands. They were never where they belonged. But he was so discreet with his unwanted overtures, Beth felt certain that no one else was aware of her plight. And she knew if she made a scene, she was going to be the one who looked like a fool.

Finally the dance was over. Beth gritted her teeth in lieu of saying what she thought of Franko as they headed back to their table. She felt certain that her stiff back and dead silence was telling him plenty. She would never make the mistake of dancing with him again. And to think, for all of five minutes she had thought this guy was Prince Charming.

Obviously she had to do something about her first impressions of men.

She was so lost in her thoughts of Franko that she was almost to their table before she realized that Jack had finally arrived. Thank heavens, she thought.

In fact, she was so happy to see him that she didn't notice the brooding expression on his face.

"I see you finally got here all safe and sound," she said, with a deep sense of relief, although her stomach was still in knots from her tug-of-war with Franko.

"I could say the same about you," he replied, a sharp, cutting edge to his tone of voice.

Beth frowned. "What do you mean? And why are you so late?"

By this time, Franko had reached their table. "Jack, my boy," he said, "I see you finally made it back."

Back, Beth thought. Now what did that mean?

But Jack was so engrossed in his conversation with Beth, he barely responded to Franko other than to say his name. He kept his glare on Beth. "Didn't you get my message?"

"Yes, I did, but—"

"I arrived at your house at seven to pick you up. But you weren't there, so I waited."

"For how long?"

"Long enough. I tried calling you on your cellular phone, but I didn't get an answer there, either. You obviously had it turned off."

"Well, I tried calling you today on yours, and I didn't get through, either," Beth replied.

"Why weren't you at home when I came to pick you up?" he asked.

"I left you a message on your answering machine at home. Didn't you get it?"

"No, I sure didn't," Jack replied with a hint of sarcasm. "Actually I haven't been home all day."

As though to ease the tension, Franko pulled out Beth's chair and she automatically sat down. "Thank you," she said to him over her shoulder. Because in that moment it was Jack alone who held her attention. "Well, that explains it then. We missed each other. I'm sorry, Jack."

Her apology seemed to have no effect on him. Instead, he smirked. "Didn't Franko tell you that I brought him here, then left just before seven to go and pick you up?"

Beth glanced up at Franko, who wore an expression of complete innocence. "No, he said that you had an errand to run. I assumed you had gotten my message, so I thought it was something else.''

''Now, Jack, my boy—'' Franko cut in ''—let's not get involved in all this detail. I can assure you, it will accomplish nothing. Apparently there was a misunderstanding of some kind. Now that we're all here at last, let's just enjoy our evening together. Besides, I want to tell you that you were right. Beth is a delight. I'm honored that she was able to join us tonight.''

Yeah, right, Beth thought, recalling what she had just gone through with him on the dance floor. She was a delightful patsy, all right. But since Jack was here now, things were definitely looking up. Surely the rest of the evening wouldn't continue to be a complete disaster. She only wished that she and Jack could have been left alone for a few seconds so they could clear up this misunderstanding between them. Normally it wasn't like him to pout over something as minor as a miscommunication. It was probably the stress of his job, and the fact that they were getting ready to put her plan into action. What else could be bothering him? she wondered.

Well, one thing was for sure. She had decided that it was pointless to tell Jack what she thought of Franko. After all, *he* had to work with the guy, she didn't. Besides, she was quite certain that Franko now knew how she felt about him, and that was the main thing.

Once they were all seated and the waiter approached, they ordered appetizers and then Franko excused himself momentarily, leaving Jack and Beth alone.

"Another rough day at the office, Jack?" Beth asked, hoping to get him to talk about whatever it was that was troubling him. He'd hardly said another word.

"Not particulary," he replied, taking a sip of his wine and not bothering to glance her way. Instead, he was working his jaw and watching the couples on the dance floor.

Beth glanced that way, too, and pretended that she hadn't noticed him practically ignoring her. But soon she couldn't take the silence, the not knowing what was wrong. She cleared her throat. "Jack, what gives? Are you tired because you didn't get a full night's sleep last night?" she asked, suddenly remembering the phone call he had made to her at three o'clock this morning. The one where he had unknowingly talked her into sleeping nude.

Franko Malone, on the other hand, could have never convinced her to sleep in the nude. Not in a million years.

But Jack, as she already knew, could talk her into anything. That was why they were such great buddies.

"No, I'm not tired," he replied flatly.

It seemed this conversation wasn't going anywhere, Beth thought. Inhaling a deep breath, she tried to think of a new angle. If she hadn't known better, she would have thought that he was upset with her. But why would he be so upset with her because of a mere miscommunication? That wasn't like Jack.

Leaning forward with a smile, Beth placed her hand on his arm. "Thanks for inviting me to join you and Franko tonight. You know how much I always enjoy the piano bar here."

"Yeah, well, when I arrived it looked to me like you were sure having yourself a grand old time on the dance floor, all right."

Stunned by the callousness of his remark, Beth straightened in her chair and gaped at him. Of all the things for Jack to have said to her. She could hardly believe that he meant it. "Is that what it looked like to you?"

"Yeah," he said sarcastically, plunking down his wineglass on the table. "That's what it looked like to me." He sat back in his chair, but continued staring straight ahead.

The very idea that Jack could have seen the dance between herself and Franko as something she had enjoyed was enough to knock the wind out of her. In fact, in her opinion, it was such an unfounded, unjust idea, that it was enough to have knocked the wind out of a hurricane. Sure, to the other guests it might have looked as though she and Franko were having an intimate dance. But Jack was her best friend. For heaven's sake, he should know her better than that. In one fraction of a second, Beth made up her mind that if Jack wanted to believe that she had been having the time of her life on the dance floor with his dear, old colleague, then he damned well could. She wasn't going to bother correcting him. Actually all she wanted now was to go home and put this entire evening behind her. It was unfolding into a nightmare.

Frankly the last forty-eight hours of her life had been a complete nightmare. At times she hadn't even known where she stood with Jack anymore. Could things possibly get any worse?

Dumb question, she told herself. Life could always get worse, and with her luck these days, it probably would.

She quickly scooped up her purse. "Look, Jack, I'm not feeling very well, so I'm going home. Give Franko my regards."

She stood up to leave.

Jack rose, too. "You can't go now," he said. "We haven't eaten yet."

"My stomach is upset. I don't think I can swallow a bite."

Suddenly Franko reappeared. "What seems to be the problem?" he asked innocently.

"Beth isn't feeling very well," Jack replied. "I think I'm going to take her home."

"I can drive myself home," Beth replied, holding a tight rein on her emotions. The last thing she wanted was for Jack—or Franko, for that matter—to know that in their own individual ways, they each had upset her. But especially Jack. She was so flabbergasted with him right now. For him to think that she had actually enjoyed Franko's advances on the dance floor…well, it was simply too much for her to deal with tonight.

Jack took hold of her arm as if he had every intention of seeing her out.

But then Franko grabbed hold of her other arm and smiled. "My dear, if you aren't feeling well, you shouldn't drive yourself home," he said. "I would be honored to escort you there. That way you won't be alone and it will put Jack's mind at ease. He'll know I'm seeing to it that you arrive home for the night all safe and sound."

Jack tightened his hold on Beth's arm. "That's quite all right, Franko. I'm used to taking care of Beth when she's ill. I'll take her home."

Franko smiled knowingly. "But why ruin your evening, Jack, my boy? You've just arrived. Besides, I'll take a taxi back here later to join you—that is, unless Beth decides in the meantime that she would like me to remain with her for the rest of the evening. In that case—"

"Forget it, Franko," Jack said almost militantly. "Beth's coming with me, and that's final."

"Look, I'm not that sick," Beth chimed in, hoping that both Jack and Franko would see how ridiculous they were being. "I can take care of myself."

"My dear Beth—" Franko began.

But Jack cut him off. "Look, Franko, the way I see it, this isn't really any of your business," he said heatedly. "Beth is my friend. So just back off." Then he turned his gaze to Beth. "Let's go. I'm taking you home."

Suddenly Beth found she'd had enough manipulation for one night. She pulled herself free from both of them and stepped back. "No one is taking me home," she replied. "I have my own car and I'm driving myself. I'm sorry if I've put a damper on the evening, but I don't think it's too late for the two of you to salvage the rest of it. Franko…uh…it was nice meeting you. Jack, I'll talk to you tomorrow. Now, good night, gentlemen."

With that, Beth turned on her heel and walked off. She was out of the restaurant and just reaching her car when Jack suddenly came up behind her.

"Beth, wait," he said breathlessly, putting his hand over hers as she was turning the key in the lock of her car door. "Something's wrong here. You've never walked out on an evening before, not even when you were sick. What's going on?"

"I don't want to talk about it right now," she said without bothering to glance back at him. After all, her feelings were hurt, and they had a right to be.

"Well, I do."

"That's too bad, Jack. Right now I just want to go home, go to bed and forget about this whole evening."

Taking her by the arms, he spun her around to face him. "That remark tells me that something is definitely wrong. I want to know what it is."

"Do you?" she said haughtily. "Or do you want to just *assume* that you know what's wrong? You seem to be quite good tonight at *assuming*."

Jack frowned. "What are you talking about?"

"Franko Malone. You assumed that I enjoyed the dance I had with him."

"Well, didn't you?"

Beth drew in a deep, calming breath. "Frankly, no."

"You didn't? Well, according to what I've seen of the guy in action, most women do."

"Then I guess I'm not like most women. I mean, he's nice and all... And he's good-looking..."

"You think he's good-looking?" Jack asked.

"Well...yeah...sort of. I thought he was a hunk, at first. But the guy has too much ego for me. But I could've handled that. He's just another one of those egotistical men that women have to deal with from time to time. It's you who upset me the most."

"Me? What did I do?" he asked, gaping at her.

"You lumped me with all those other women whom you claim have fallen all over themselves because of Franko and then you didn't even give me a chance to defend myself."

"Look, I'm sorry," he said meaningfully. "Actually I don't suppose I was thinking at all. I saw his arms around you, and it looked to me like—"

"Well, you were wrong," Beth cut in.

"He wanted to go home with you," Jack said.

"Did I let him?" she asked heatedly.

Jack smirked at his own ridiculous assumptions. "No, you didn't."

"Thank you for finally recognizing that fact," she said patronizingly.

"I know I had that coming, but the truth is, I didn't want to see you get hurt. The guy's a wolf in sheep's clothing."

"We're not in grade school anymore, Jack. I'm a big girl now. I can take care of myself."

Of course, at the time when she had been fighting off Franko's advances on and off the dance floor, that wasn't exactly what she had been telling herself. She had been in a near panic for Jack to save her.

"Let's just forget about what happened tonight," she said, suddenly straightening his tie with the ease and self-assurance of a close friend. A slight smile turned up the corners of her mouth. "I'm exhausted anyway. I really should get to bed early. But you go back inside the restaurant with Franko and have yourselves a good time. I want you to."

Suddenly, from out of nowhere, the thought of all those women sitting at the piano bar, hungry for attention and just waiting for a nice, good-looking guy like Jack to arrive, made her stomach knot up again. It was the strangest thing. She didn't like the idea of him dancing with all those other women. "Just don't stay out too late," she said in a motherly fashion, as a kind of paralyzing fear gripped hold of her heart. "You probably have a long day ahead of you tomorrow."

"Yeah, as a matter of fact, I do. I think I'll just eat the appetizers we ordered and then go on home. If Franko isn't ready to return to his hotel by that time, he can always take a taxi later."

"Now that sounds like a smart idea," she said, smiling at him. It wasn't much assurance for all the possessive thoughts going through her head, but it was better than nothing.

Jack grinned at her. "Look, everything happened so fast a while ago that I didn't get a chance to tell you that you really look great tonight," he said, his eyes drifting slowly down her body.

An intense heat rose up in her loins and channeled its way up to her cheeks, causing her to feel all flustered inside. "Really?"

"Do me a favor, okay?" he drawled, his eyes coming back up to meet hers. "Wear this outfit the next time we go out to dinner together."

"Okay," she said without argument. Frankly, in that moment, she would have done just about anything for him. Anything at all.

He leaned forward and kissed her lightly on the lips.

"Why did you do that?" she asked.

"I don't know," he said. "I just felt like it. Look, I might call you tonight when I get in, just to see how you're feeling."

Her heart fluttered. "I'm perfectly fine, Jack. Really, I am."

"I know. But do you mind if I call you anyway?"

She remembered his phone call from the night before, and grinned. "No, I don't mind."

From the look in his eyes, she knew that he was remembering it. He grinned back.

Then he opened her car door, and she got inside and drove away. But as the miles passed, Beth realized she could hardly wait until he called her later on that night. It wasn't just that she was slightly uneasy knowing that he would be out on the town with someone as notorious with women as Franko Malone, but she was honestly missing him already.

But Beth never got her phone call that night from Jack. By morning, she didn't know if she should be worried sick or just plain angry at him for causing her to stay awake most of the night, waiting for her telephone to ring. This was the second night in a row that she hadn't had enough sleep because of him. It was getting to be a habit.

Not that she seriously thought she had a right to be truly angry with him. The fact that he hadn't called her was…well…nothing, really. He certainly didn't owe her an explanation. When it came right down to it, he was an unattached male who could do what he darned well pleased. He wasn't her property, after all. It wasn't as if she was his wife or anything. Not yet, anyway. But the thought that he could have gone home from that restaurant last night with some woman and there was absolutely nothing she could do about it was suddenly driving her plum crazy.

Halfheartedly, she dragged herself out of bed, made a pot of coffee and drank two cups.

And then her phone rang. She practically dove forward to answer it.

"Hello."

"Beth—"

"Jack! Where are you?"

So much for playing it cool with him, she thought.

There was a hesitation. "It's a long story, Beth. Look, do you have coffee made?"

She glanced over at the pot of hot brew sitting on her countertop. "Uh…yeah…sure."

"Mind if I come by? I could use a cup."

"Jack, what's wrong?"

"Look, I'll explain when I get there, if it's all right that I come?"

"Of course."

"I'll be there in ten minutes."

"Okay." She was going to hang up the phone when she heard him say, "Oh—and, Beth…"

She pushed the receiver back against her ear. "Yes, Jack?"

"I'm sorry that I didn't call you last night. I… uh…I got tied up."

"Oh," Beth said, her heart pounding in her throat. "What time did you finally get in?"

"Truthfully, I never made it in," he said. "That's what I want to tell you about."

Beth's heart sank to the floor.

Now she knew why she'd had all those dreadful—almost jealous—feelings during the night. Jack had met someone while he was out with Franko. Someone special enough to keep him away from home all night long, and somehow she had sensed it was happening.

And now he wanted to come by this morning and tell his good old friend Beth all about it. How lucky could she be?

Actually she had always suspected that this day might come sooner or later. But why did it have to be now, when she had other plans for him in the next couple of months?

Besides, just what did he think he was going to do with some other woman while he was married to her, for heaven's sake? Had he even stopped to think about that?

But the truth was, Jack's happiness was just as important to her as her own. If he'd finally met someone who somehow captivated his heart, she was going to smile and be happy for him. Even if it put a major kink in her plans. Even if she had to suffer in silence.

With that thought in mind, she forced a smile to her face. "Well, hurry up. I can't wait to hear what happened to you last night."

"You're going to be so surprised, Beth, you won't believe it," he said.

"Oh, I bet I will," she said, her stomach turning into knots. Because she was already convinced that she knew.

If only she could somehow convince her heart not to care that she did.

Jack arrived at her door twelve minutes and thirty-seven seconds later. He looked terrible. His suit coat and his tie were missing, and his white shirt looked as though he'd slept in it—which, of course, Beth immediately realized, was obviously wishful thinking on her part. He was unshaven and he looked exhausted.

"My God, Jack, what happened to you?" Beth asked.

"Could I use your bathroom to wash up?"

"Uh…sure."

He went straight to the hall bath and closed the

door. When he came out a few minutes later, he'd rolled up the sleeves of his white shirt. His hair was wet and Beth knew he'd splashed cold water on his face. She had already poured him a cup of coffee, so he sat down at her breakfast table and took a sip. Beth waited in silence, anxiously wanting to hear what had happened to him, and yet not wanting to hear it at all. He would tell her, she knew, in his own good time.

Finally he looked across the table at her. "Do you know why I didn't call you last night?"

Beth's gut knotted. "Well, you said you never made it home."

"I didn't. But do you know why?"

Beth held on tight to her emotions. "I can only suppose it was because you and Franko were having such a good time out on the town."

He smirked. "Yeah, right. We had a time, all right. We spent most of it at the city jail."

Beth gaped at him. "You got arrested?"

"I didn't," he said, taking another sip from his coffee. "But Franko and this other guy did."

"What other guy?"

"The guy that slugged Franko after Franko made a pass at his wife."

"You're kidding."

"Franko slugged the guy back and the next thing I knew, they were being thrown out of the restaurant. But that was only the beginning. The guy jumped Franko in the parking lot and then they really got into it. I finally broke them apart, but it was too late by then. The police had already been called and both of them were put under arrest. I had to go down to the station as a witness and tell my side of the story. Turned out Franko didn't have any identification on him, so that became a problem. Our boss had to be called in, and now Franko is in trouble with his job, too. I'm telling you, it was a mess, Beth. I was just so glad you had already gone home.''

"Wow…'' Beth said, relieved beyond belief to finally hear what had really happened to him last night. He obviously hadn't slept a wink, but that was okay. He hadn't exactly spent a romantic night in another woman's arms, either. And that was something important for her to remember. "Where's Franko now?'' she asked.

"He's still in jail.''

"Oh, Jack, you poor guy,'' she said, reaching across the table and covering his hand. "To think you had to baby-sit all night long down at city jail for a grown man who knew better, but still chose to get himself into trouble anyway. Did you get any sleep at all?''

"No, but since Franko ended up being such an unexpected problem for both me and the company, my boss gave me the day off.'' He glanced back in the direction of her bedroom. "In fact, I wouldn't have a problem crawling into your bed right now and falling asleep.''

"You mean, here? At my house?''

He shrugged off her surprise. "It was just a thought. I didn't mean it, Beth.''

"Well…'' she said, actually giving his remark

some added thought. "It probably isn't such a bad idea, after all. You know, you just might have trouble getting some rest at your place. Once your co-workers find out what happened to you and Franko last night, they'll be calling you, or coming by for details. It's human nature," she said with a shrug. "Unfortunately, everyone loves a juicy story. But, look, I'm going to be leaving for work soon anyway. Put your car in my garage so no one will know that you're here, and the house is yours for the day."

Jack grew thoughtful. "You know, that doesn't sound like such a bad idea."

"It's a great idea," Beth said, giving his hand one final squeeze before getting up from the table and heading toward her bedroom. "Now go and move your car inside my garage. I'm going to start getting ready for work. I'll be in the shower, but I'll be out soon, if you need anything."

With that, she turned and went down the hall.

Jack stood up from the breakfast table and watched Beth head toward her bedroom. How he loved that woman—only, not in the way that a man loved a woman, he corrected himself quickly. But as a best friend. Her pampering ways had a healing effect on him.

In fact, the idea of spending the day alone in her house, sleeping in her soft bed, tucking her sweet smelling pillows under his head was, indeed, a pleasurable thought. One he had no intention of passing up.

Placing his empty coffee cup in the sink, Jack

strolled outside to put his car in her garage. Instinctively he knew that he was heading straight into more trouble than he could possibly imagine with her, but he couldn't see how he could turn back now.

Nor, if truth be told, did he really want to.

Chapter Seven

Beth was out of the shower in five minutes. After drying herself off and wrapping her wet hair in a towel, she slipped on her blue cotton bathrobe.

She still thought the idea of having Jack stay at her house today in order to get the rest he obviously needed was a good one, and she was glad she had thought of it. In fact, she now realized that she should have thought of getting the guest bedroom ready for him before showering. He could have been asleep by now. But since she hadn't thought of it until this moment, she just hoped that he hadn't fallen asleep while waiting for her at her kitchen table. She would hate having to wake him up, when she knew that he would only be going right back to sleep again.

Securing her robe by tying the belt at her waist, Beth walked out of the bathroom. Her plan, of course, was to go straight to the kitchen where she thought Jack would still be sitting, no doubt waiting for her to get out of the shower so she could help him get settled in her extra bedroom. But as she passed the foot of her bed, she suddenly realized that Jack was lying across it. She came to an abrupt halt and gaped.

He was sound asleep. Just like that. While she was in the shower. She could tell he was out cold by his low, steady breathing. Not only was that a dead give-away, but he hadn't moved a muscle since she'd spotted him. He was lying flat on his back, his arms thrown out, his legs hanging over the side of her mattress. His feet were placed flat on the floor. Obviously he'd lain across her bed, waiting for her to come out from the shower, and had gone out like a light instead.

Now what was she going to do with him? Beth wondered. There was no way she could carry him into the next bedroom. Not by herself. Besides, she would wake him up if she tried, and she didn't want to do that. Poor guy, this was the first shut-eye he'd had in over twenty-four hours. Not to mention the fact that he was still trying to recover from jet lag.

Besides, this was her house, wasn't it? She could allow him to sleep anywhere she wanted. The fact was, he wasn't hurting anyone by being in her bed. She wasn't even going to be home while he slept.

Should she just leave him sprawled out on top of her mattress like that? she debated. At some point, wouldn't he get chilled, or perhaps get a cramped muscle?

Did she dare try to move him, though?

His shoes, she thought suddenly. The least she could do was remove his shoes. Stepping forward, Beth dropped to her knees at his feet. In the next moment she removed one shiny black loafer from his foot, then his black sock, and then his other black loafer and sock. Now he was barefoot, and she felt almost certain he was more comfortable. She rose from the floor and smiled to herself.

Then her eyes skidded over his sleeping form.

His belt, she realized a second later. She needed to loosen his belt, too. No doubt he would breathe easier and, therefore, rest better. She quickly leaned over him, bracing herself on one hand while she worked the buckle until it finally gave way, causing his belt to relax around his waist.

Straightening up and breathing a sigh of relief, she was certain he was going to be much more comfortable now. And it was time she finished getting herself ready to go to work. She had another early appointment this morning for a potential sale on a house. The couple involved wanted to meet with her at eight forty-five. That was less than two hours away.

She was turning to go back into the bathroom to blow-dry her hair when for no particular reason, she caught sight of his bare feet…his bare toes. Only this time, she didn't think they were going to be okay. In fact, she became somewhat concerned. With her central cooling unit pushing cold air into the rooms of her house all day long, those bare little darlings might very well end up getting cold. She stood there, eyeing them, while she twitched her mouth back and forth, debating whether or not she should put his socks back on.

Instead, she came to another conclusion. One along the same line of thinking, only on a much larger scale. It wasn't just his feet that needed to be protected against the cool environment of her home, but his whole body. He needed to be under the covers on her bed. But how could she make that happen? She couldn't exactly pull the covers over him when he was lying on top of them, still wearing his pants and shirt. Not only would his clothing be a complete hindrance to him while he slept under the covers, but they would end up being even more of a mess than they already were. She was a stickler about things like that. Just how difficult, she wondered, would it be to get him undressed down to his shorts and then get him under the covers of her bed?

She would never know unless she gave it a try.

She decided to start with his pants.

Then she quickly decided to remove his shirt instead.

Beth crawled on the bed alongside him, breathed in deeply and began to unbutton his shirt.

She did it carefully, slowly remembering the evening only two nights ago when she and Jack had gone out to Wilibee's pond. He'd taken his shirt off that night. So had she. Swallowing hard, she fumbled with the last button that held the shirt together and then slowly dragged the two sides apart. Her breath locked in her throat. Heaven help her, but he was so beautiful.

•

She couldn't help herself. She ran the tips of her fingers lightly over his taut skin, feeling his rib cage, the flatness of his abdomen, the tightness of his nipples. His belly button was peeking out above the waistline of his pants, and Beth got the sudden naughty urge to kiss him there.

She broke out in a cold sweat instead. The kind that had a way of making her realize how close she had just come to making a complete fool of herself. She couldn't believe she'd actually thought of doing something that scandalous to Jack. For heaven's sake, what had she been thinking?

She quickly refocused on her task, turning her attention to the waistband of his trousers, and quickly unfastening it. Then, fumbling her way down to his zipper, she began tugging lightly on the pull tab.

Suddenly her wrists were encircled in a viselike grip.

Startled, she sucked in a deep breath and cut her eyes to look at Jack. He was staring at her. "What in the hell are you doing?"

"I...uh...I...was putting you to bed."

He blinked twice and then stared at her blankly.

She glanced down at what she'd been trying to do—dear Lord, she had him all undressed—and then looked back up to meet his expression. She was lucky he was her best friend. Otherwise, he might have misconstrued her intentions. "I...uh...was trying to undress you without waking you up so I could get you under the covers." She frowned. "I guess I goofed, huh?"

It seemed to take him a moment to absorb everything she said, but when finally he did, he smiled and began to methodically move her into a position where she ended up sitting on top of him, her legs folded under on each side of him. "There," he said, apparently pleased with where he had her.

She was sitting on his stomach.

Hot, naked skin against hot, naked skin.

The thought of it took her breath away.

And then he untied the sash at her waist and opened up her robe until she was completely naked to his viewing.

Beth's breath locked in her throat. "Oh, no, Jack, now I know we shouldn't be doing this."

"And I shouldn't have caught you undressing me, but I did," he countered. Then he reached out and caressed her breasts, and Beth thought the top of her head would explode from the crazed emotions surging upward through her body.

"This is insane, Jack," she said breathlessly.

"I know," he replied in that deep, gruff-sounding voice of his. He pulled her to him and kissed her hungrily between her breasts. "But do you honestly want me to stop now?" he asked, pulling away and looking deep into her eyes.

Beth was in a tug-of-war with herself. Of course, she didn't want him to stop. Not ever. Having him touch her like this was pure heaven. But not stopping him had serious consequences. Consequences that they might not be able to live with tomorrow. This moment wasn't just about sex, and they both knew it.

This was about need…and abandonment…and something else that went much deeper than they would ever admit. It was about desire and a deep down hunger that was eating at her soul. This was taboo territory for her—for them, no doubt about it.

She had been right a moment ago. This was insane.

Suddenly Jack rolled over and now was on top of her. He began kissing her breasts, her neck, her lips. He used his tongue…his mouth. He rubbed the side of his face against one of her breasts. It was rough… exciting…sexy. Beth was on fire. She wanted him. She wanted all of him.

"Jack…please…wait…" she said, fighting for control. "I have to get to work on time."

"I could get you pregnant right now—this very minute," he whispered near her ear. "Just think about it, Beth. All you have to do is say the word." His hand slipped between her legs, and Beth thought she would surely die from the sheer pleasure of his touch.

She wanted it all so bad—him…a baby. "But we're not married yet," she heard herself say.

Abruptly he stopped the delicious things he was doing to her body and gazed deeply, meaningfully into her eyes as only her dearest, most trusted friend would have done. "Does having a marriage certificate first really mean that much to you?"

Beth knew the answer to that one. It had been a part of her soul for too long for her not to. "Yes."

"And would you regret it later on if you decided to break your own rules?"

"Are we talking about what's happening between us right now?" she asked, wide-eyed.

"Yeah," he said gruffly. "We're talking about what's happening between us right now."

Beth turned her face away from him. She needed a moment where she wasn't being completely influenced by his penetrating gaze. Finally she nodded. "Yeah, probably."

For a brief second, he didn't move a muscle. Then, suddenly, he lifted himself from on top of her and said, "Okay, then. That does it. We wait."

A sudden splash of cold, harsh air rushed over her nakedness. Having moved to the foot of her bed, Jack gazed down at her and said, "I can't believe I just said that."

Finally, though, after apparently coming to terms with it, he grinned. "Go on. Get out of here, Beth, and go to work before I change my mind about this whole matter and get back into bed with you. I'd sure hate for you not to be able to live with yourself if we did something rash. Besides," he continued, that smile of his easing all the way across his face, "I thought you said I could get some rest around here. Where's all the quiet you promised me?"

Beth pulled her robe closed and gaped at him. "Look, if you're trying to imply what just happened was my fault—"

He raised his hand to calm her. "I didn't say that. But just who was caught undressing who when I woke up?" he said smugly.

Beth sat up at the end of her bed. "I wasn't undressing you, at least not for the reason you think."

Jack came closer and lifted her chin until she was looking at him. Then he smiled into her eyes. "I know why you were undressing me, Beth. And thanks."

With Jack looking at her so intently Beth couldn't think of anything to say.

"You know what I think?" he continued. "I think we need to get married as soon as possible. It's time we get you pregnant so that things can get back to normal between us."

Beth was still so shaken from their behavior a moment ago that she wasn't thinking quite straight. But she had enough sense about her to know that Jack was probably right. They had to do something about what was going on between them. "I haven't had a chance to tell you yet, but I found a Justice of the Peace who can marry us on Saturday."

"Good," he replied. "It's about time we get this show on the road."

For the record, Beth was feeling the same sense of urgency that he obviously did. And, perhaps, Jack knew what he was talking about. They had already come so far, so fast since she'd asked him to help her with her plan that maybe a temporary marriage between them might be the only way to appease this...this whatever it was that was happening between them now. Frankly she was convinced it had more to do with hormones and babies—and Mother Nature playing her mating call—than anything else.

They both knew what she wanted from Jack. It was only natural that their sex drives eventually come into play.

With the tense seconds from a moment ago behind them, Jack walked up to the side of her bed, dropped his pants as though it were nothing, pulled off his shirt and then got between the cool sheets on her bed. Beth stood and watched as he took his own good time fluffing up her pillows.

"Nighty-night," he finally said. "I'll see you when you get back this afternoon."

He started to turn his back to her, but then he stopped halfway and glanced back over his shoulder. "Oh, and Beth…" he added. "If you don't mind, bring home Chinese tonight. I've got this sudden craving for fried rice."

And then he rolled over and closed his eyes. It wasn't long, Beth knew, before he was asleep.

Just like that, she thought to herself.

It was as though it was no big deal that he was her best friend and was sleeping in her bed. And, truthfully, it really wasn't.

But it should have been a big deal that just minutes ago he had brought out such powerful feelings in her that she could have easily lost herself to him forever.

But that hadn't seemed to phase him any more than sleeping in her bed did. At least, not as it had her.

When Beth finally arrived at her office just past eight o'clock, she called Karen first thing to see if she would stand as a witness when she and Jack took their vows. Of course, her friend was delighted at the prospect. Beth knew she would be.

Then with her early-morning appointment in mind, Beth rose from behind her desk, picked up her purse and went to meet the young couple who were looking to buy a house. The rest of her day was pretty routine as well, and by five o'clock that afternoon what had happened between her and Jack in her bedroom that morning seemed almost like a dream.

She picked up Chinese on her way home from work.

Jack's car was still parked in her garage when she drove in. She entered the house through the back door and flicked on the kitchen light. All was quiet. She went straight to her bedroom and saw that Jack was still sound asleep in her bed. Trying to be as quiet as possible, she got a pair of shorts and a shirt from inside her closet, then went to her bathroom and shut the door so she wouldn't disturb him while she changed from her work clothes.

But when she came out of the bathroom, he had rolled over and was lying flat on his back. His eyes were open and he was obviously waiting for her. "Hi," he said, his voice deep and rich from sleep. "Just got in?"

"Not long ago," she answered, keeping her voice steady while she carefully placed her work clothes back on their hangers inside her closet. She told herself that she was not going to look at him, regardless of how much she wanted to. Under normal circumstances, having Jack Kincaid lying half-asleep in her

bed would have been no big deal. But according to
the way her heart was suddenly pounding, no longer
was this a normal circumstance for her. Frankly she
had come too close to abandoning herself to him in
that same bed earlier that morning for her to be completely at ease. No way could she let her guard down
like that again. There was too much at stake.

Jack turned on the lamp next to her bed.

The sudden splash of light drew Beth's immediate
attention, and she automatically glanced over her
shoulder in time to see him sit up in bed. So much
for self-control, she thought a second later. The sheet
that had been covering him when she came in a few
moments ago had now slipped down to his waist, and
his bare chest made a delicious picture against the
backdrop of her overstuffed headboard. Her stomach
bottomed out.

It was time they moved to her kitchen to have supper, Beth thought.

Suddenly Jack threw back the covers and swung
his feet over the side of the bed. After a big yawn,
he stretched his arms over his head and said, "I slept
like a baby."

Beth followed his actions, not even realizing that
some wanton part of herself was absorbing every
move he made.

She was still watching him when he began bounc-
ing on the end of her bed as if he was testing it out.
"You know," he began, "when the time comes, I'm
really going to enjoy this mattress," he said.

Crisscrossing her arms under her breasts, Beth

stood and watched him check out the durability of her bedsprings. She knew what he was getting at, but she wasn't taking the bait.

"I brought home Chinese," she said flatly, determined to keep the subject going in that direction. "I'm hungry. Let's go eat."

One thing she could always be sure of about Jack. The kinds of things that always seemed to rattle her the most never seemed to bother him at all. That was probably what made them perfect friends.

After putting on his pants, Jack helped her make up her bed, then he went to take a shower in her bathroom. While he was doing that, Beth went into the kitchen and set the table.

A few minutes later Jack entered the room, fully dressed, and sat down with her to eat. "I had a dream last night," he said, spooning a heap of fried rice onto his plate. "I dreamed we had a big wedding on Saturday."

"Well, at least you got the Saturday part right," Beth said, dunking her egg roll into a mixture of sweet-and-sour sauce.

"I think we should have a big wedding—invite all our friends," he said, setting his fork down. "You've always wanted one, haven't you?"

"Get real, Jack," she said. "Saturday is only five days away. There isn't time to plan that kind of wedding. Besides, who needs it? We'll be divorced before we know it."

Jack leaned forward. "Which, in a way, is exactly why we should have one. It's all going to be over and done with so fast, I think we ought to have some fun with it. Besides, how much trouble can it be to plan a wedding that will include our friends.''

Beth could only gape at him. Obviously he had no idea.

''Look,'' he said, ''we can set up everything in your backyard. Matt's cousin can do the catering. And doesn't June play the organ and sing at her church? She can do the wedding march, or whatever that song is called. We'll have champagne, too. It'll be a blast.''

''I don't know…'' Beth said hesitantly.

''Come on. Be a sport. Let's make it into a party.''

''What about our parents?'' Beth asked, after giving his idea some consideration and deciding it might be kind of fun, after all. ''If we invite our friends, shouldn't we invite them, too?''

Jack frowned. ''We'd have to do all kinds of explaining to them. That alone could take five days.''

''You're right,'' Beth replied. ''Maybe it isn't such a good idea to invite them after all.''

''Let's keep the guest list limited to just our closest friends,'' Jack said. ''Those whom we know will understand our reasons for doing what we're doing.''

Beth smiled knowingly. ''I agree.''

''Okay, then. I'll take care of the catering, the champagne and the music.''

''And I'll take care of ordering a larger cake—I'd already ordered a small one for us,'' Beth said. ''And I'll get all the decorations, too. And I'll ask Karen to be my maid of honor, instead of just our witness.''

''I can get Chuck to stand as my best man.''

"Wow," Beth said, "looks like we've already got it all covered."

"See," Jack said. "I told you all those details would be nothing to get done."

Beth smiled. "It's so good to know that when life gets a little crazy, I can always depend on you to settle things down for me, Jack."

"Hey," he said playfully, "what's a good friend for?"

What, indeed? Beth thought, gazing at him with a deep-down pride that came from knowing that he was her best friend.

She and Jack had something really special, all right, and she was going to do all she could to see to it that it never changed.

Chapter Eight

Beth found it difficult to believe that today was her wedding day and that within the next hour she and Jack were going to be married.

The past five days leading up to this moment had been hectic. When she and Jack had decided to have a bigger wedding, they naively thought they had all the details covered and that everything would automatically fall into place for them, but they had been mistaken. Nothing had gone according to their plans. The caterer, the baker, the photographer—all had gone wrong. So wrong, in fact, that by mid-Thursday morning they had come close to canceling their plans and instead have a simple ceremony, after all.

But their friends had stepped forward to offer their assistance and somehow, in just three short days, they had been able to organize everything for the big occasion. Now it seemed that their wedding day was going to be something to remember. She'd even managed to find herself a white lace, floor-length bridal gown, and a head veil that she adored. At their friends' insistence, both she and Jack had taken off a couple of days from their jobs for a brief honeymoon in New Orleans. Hopefully—and she had her fingers crossed, to be sure—she would be pregnant by the time they got back. Only she couldn't let herself worry about that right now. One step at a time, she kept saying to herself.

In fact, as far as she currently knew, Jack was still out shopping for the wedding bands they had almost forgotten in all the mad rush until he'd thought of them just a couple of hours ago. But according to Karen, who was taking her role as Beth's maid of honor quite seriously, everything was on schedule. In fact, she had just slipped into Beth's bedroom for the hundredth time to assure her that Jack was already dressed in his black tux and would be ready to begin the ceremony the moment he arrived at her house. Karen informed Beth that he had just called from a jeweler's across town to say that he'd found what he was looking for and was on his way. Beth breathed a sigh of relief.

Not that she thought it was necessary for her and Jack to have matching wedding rings. It was Jack who had insisted on it. And these days, it seemed, when Jack put his mind to something, heaven help them all, but there was no use trying to talk him out of it.

She hadn't seen Jack since yesterday. And she'd

talked to him only once. Their friends had made sure that the two of them followed the age-old custom where the groom doesn't get to see the bride on their wedding day until the start of the ceremony. In fact, Karen and some of the others were making a big hoopla over the whole thing, keeping Beth hidden away in her bedroom, claiming it was tradition and all. They were acting as though they thought her and Jack's marriage was going to be forever, when, of course, they all knew better. Nonetheless, they seemed to be having a good time helping her with her wedding plans and, in truth, so was Beth. Jack seemed to be pleased with the way things were going, too. The day was turning out to be far more than she had ever dreamed at such short notice. In fact, she and Jack had changed their minds at the last minute and invited their parents to come, too. According to Karen, they were all presently seated in her backyard, waiting for the ceremony to begin.

Suddenly Beth's bedroom door swung open and a moment later Karen stuck her head inside. "He's here," she said.

"Jack?" Beth asked, her heart pounding.

"Yes. Oh—and Beth, your rings are really beautiful."

"Are they?" Beth asked, feeling almost heady with excitement.

For what seemed like the hundredth time that day, Karen rushed into the room and hugged her. "I'm so happy for you, I could cry," she said, sniffing up several loose tears.

"How does Jack look?" Beth asked, taking a deep, steadying breath, although she had little doubt that his white-and-black tuxedo combination made him an exciting groom for any bride to be.

"Handsome—but nervous," Karen said, wiping at her tears.

"Is he?"

"Just a little. How are you?"

"I've got butterflies in my stomach, but I'm okay," Beth replied.

"Well, they sent me in here to see if you were ready to begin. Are you?"

"I think so," Beth said. Then, suddenly feeling the need to make her cause known one last time before proceeding with the final step, she grabbed hold of Karen's arm. "All of this is just temporary, you know."

"Yeah, sure, I know," Karen replied absently, the whole time inspecting Beth to make sure that the bride's dress and veil were perfectly aligned for her walk down the aisle.

Beth licked her lips. "Karen, listen to me. Before you know it, Jack and I will be divorced and everything will be back to normal again. I want you to remember that, okay?"

"Okay," Karen replied apathetically. Finally finishing her task of inspecting Beth's appearance, she glanced up and smiled in a way that told Beth she hadn't heard a single word. "Ready for your big moment?" Karen asked.

Beth's breath locked in her throat. Was she?

Of course, she was.

"Yes," she said.

"Then I'll go tell them we're ready to start," Karen said, hurrying out of the room. A few moments later Beth's father knocked on her bedroom door and then stepped inside. After telling her what a beautiful bride she made, he offered her his arm and said, "Everyone's waiting for you." Beth heard the organist begin playing the song that signalled it was time for the bride to make her appearance.

Inhaling a deep breath, she took her father's arm. He led her to her backyard where her family and friends—and her groom—were all anxiously waiting for her.

Before she knew it, she was walking toward Jack, with row after row of their family and friends watching her from portable folding chairs set up for the occasion. At the head of it all was a tall trellis, decorated in English ivy and white satin ribbons. And, of course, the Justice of the Peace was standing dead center. To her left near the front, she saw that her mother was crying. To her right she saw Jack's parents and then noticed that his mother was dabbing at the corners of her eyes, too. Then she saw Karen. Thank goodness, she was smiling—well, sort of.

And then she saw Jack.

Thank goodness for Jack.

He was looking at her with an infectious, heartfelt grin. He didn't even have to say the words, because somehow, just by gazing into his eyes, Beth knew that he thought she was the most beautiful bride he'd ever seen. And for the first time in what had seemed like endless moments of walking through a haze, Beth actually felt like…well, like maybe she was going to make it through this day after all.

A smile to match the one on his face sprang to her lips, and then suddenly it was as though the whole world was smiling at her. At them. She felt happy…contented…at peace with herself. As though she knew she was doing the right thing. After all, Jack was the perfect choice to be the father of her child.

When Beth and her father reached the end of the aisle, he kissed her on the cheek and then gave her away to Jack. Suddenly the moment was so intense, so all-consuming, that tears sprang to her eyes.

"I have you now," Jack whispered to her teasingly. "And you look so beautiful, I just might not ever let you go."

"You don't have any choice," Beth replied, gazing up at him, her heart pounding in her throat. "It's already in the rules that you have to."

"But I don't always follow the rules," he said, his eyes twinkling with merriment.

"Oh, but I do," Beth replied.

He just laughed at that.

Joining hands, they turned toward the Justice of the Peace so that the ceremony could begin. As it turned out, Karen was right about Jack's choice of wedding rings. They had an antique gold finish and were quite lovely. He obviously had known what she liked.

Before long, they had said their vows and were pronounced husband and wife. Jack took her into his arms and kissed her thoroughly, passionately, until everyone in attendance burst into a loud, joyous applause. When he finally ended the kiss, the intensity of his gaze told her that he had known exactly what he was doing. He had wanted to prove a point to her and, by golly, he had. He released her and grinned.

"Wow, that was some kiss," Karen stated. "Are you okay?"

"I'm fine," Beth said in a shaky voice. She composed herself enough to greet their families and friends who were coming up to them now, slapping Jack on the back and congratulating them.

Lifting her eyebrows in question, Karen leaned in close to Beth's ear. "Are you sure you aren't pregnant already? That was some kiss you just got."

Heaven help her, but Beth knew there was no way she could deny that. Jack's kiss had been so thorough, so earth-shattering in its quest that she'd felt it all the way down to the tips of her toes. In fact, her wobbly knees were testimony to the fact that her whole body had been affected. Not to mention, her head was still reeling.

What in the world had gotten into Jack lately anyway? Sometimes he acted...well, he acted as if what was happening to them was for real. As if their marriage was going to last forever.

But, of course, it wasn't, and he knew it.

Then again, Jack could be such a teaser. He was probably just playing his part as her groom to the hilt.

The main thing was, they had to come out of this as still being the best of friends.

So far, so good.

Now if she could just make it through the next part of her plan—which, of course, was the sex part. It wouldn't be long now before she would know for sure, one way or the other.

But she and Jack had to get through the reception first, and then they had a two-hour road trip to New Orleans by limo. According to her calculations, "D" Day was only a few hours away.

Soon she and Jack were cutting their wedding cake, while posing for the photographer every step along the way. Jack told her that she would be glad later on to have these pictures to show her child, and Beth agreed.

The next thing she knew, Jack was telling her that the limo he'd hired to drive them to New Orleans was waiting outside. They went into her bedroom and quickly changed into the outfits they planned to travel in. With the constant flow of interruptions at Beth's bedroom door, they hurriedly shed one set of clothing for the other without worrying too much about the intimate nature of getting undressed in front of each other. They did it automatically, without any thought.

A short time later, loaded up with their luggage, a couple of bottles of champagne and a few sandwiches from their reception table, they climbed into the back seat of the white limousine while their parents and friends practically drowned them in birdseed. It was a relief when the limo door finally closed and she and Jack were suddenly alone. But no sooner had they settled themselves than they were waving goodbye to everyone from their rearview window as the limousine pulled away.

Beth was both exhausted and exhilarated, from the day's events. She leaned back in her seat and took a deep breath.

With a grin on his face, Jack popped the cork on the first bottle of champagne and poured them each a glass. "To a long and happy mating season," he said, clicking his glass to hers.

Beth smiled at first, but when she realized what he had said, her mouth dropped open.

"Go easy on the champagne," he stated a moment later, completely ignoring her expression as he took her glass from her hand. "I want a conscious, consenting woman on my hands when we reach our hotel."

"Jack, for heaven's sake…"

He took one of her hands into his. "Hey, I can see that you're nervous. Your fingers are like ice." He rubbed them briskly between his two hands.

He was right. She was a nervous wreck.

Now that all the commotion of the wedding and reception was behind her, she had nothing to think of but what lay ahead of her in New Orleans. And what lay ahead of her was…well…their honeymoon. Maybe if what they were going to be doing together once they got there wasn't such a planned thing…maybe if she hadn't known that everything they had done so far centered around that one particular happening, it wouldn't have been so nerve-racking. But as it was, she was a mess.

Her eyes lifted to meet his, and he flashed her one of his infectious smiles. And, somehow, it made her feel more relaxed.

"You've come this far, Beth. Don't worry, you'll make it through the rest of it, too."

She felt breathless. "I know I will. I'm just so glad you're here with me, Jack."

He laughed lightly. "Don't you worry," he said, slipping his arm around her shoulders. "I plan to be with you every step of the way."

That, needless to say, was the reason she needed his help in the first place. This level of her plan was, indeed, turning into a catch-22. Suddenly it seemed that where Jack was concerned, she was damned if she did and damned if she didn't.

"Look," he said, "let's forget about, you know, the sex part for right now and just enjoy the ride. We're on our honeymoon, for heaven's sake. How often does that happen in one's lifetime? In mine, it's going to be a first and last. After I'm done with this marriage, I plan to stay a bachelor."

"Good for you," Beth said, taking back her glass of champagne from him for a long swallow. Truthfully there was a part of her that didn't want to think of him belonging to another woman in that way anyway. Jack was her friend. And for the time being, at least, he was also her husband. She handed Jack back her empty glass, snuggled up in the seat next to him and placed her head on his shoulder.

"Sleepy?" he asked, looking at her with a tender expression on his face.

"Mmm... Just a little tired."

He placed his fingers under her chin and then kissed her lightly on the lips. "Then close your eyes and rest for a while."

"I think I will," she mumbled, shutting them.

And without realizing it, she fell asleep.

Jack glanced down at his bride and smiled knowingly to himself.

That was one way of getting Beth to their hotel room in New Orleans without her becoming a complete basket case in the process, he thought.

Now if he could just keep himself from being overly anxious to make her his own.

It won't be long now, he told himself, hoping to pacify his growing desire.

Only it was too late for that. He was beyond help.

He had been waiting for this moment his whole life.

He hadn't really known it until now.

Beth was damned lucky she had fallen asleep. Otherwise, he might have decided to take her right here and now. Some friend he was turning out to be. And then it hit him. He wasn't just her friend. He was her husband.

Beth's eyes fluttered open at the sound of her name.

"Beth..." she heard Jack say again. "We're at the hotel now. It's time to wake up."

Wake up? Beth thought, coming straight up in her seat. She stared wide-eyed at her surroundings, now cloaked in darkness except for the streetlights overhead and the few neon signs she saw scattered down the block. Sure enough, the sights…the smells…the whole atmosphere told her that they had arrived at their destination. There was no other city in the world quite like New Orleans. It was all one big cocktail, where the old mixed in with the new, where the supernatural mixed in with reality and gave the city a mythical heartbeat all its own.

She climbed out of the limousine at the curb on Esplanade Street and led the way inside the lobby of their small hotel located just off the French Quarter's mainstream. Jack followed closely at her heels while directing the bellman where to place their luggage. The young Creole woman at the front desk giggled the whole time she registered them as newlyweds, and for Beth it brought the whole dire situation back into focus for her. She and Jack would soon be going to bed together. She couldn't help but wonder when the time came who was going to be the one with enough courage to make that all important first move?

Looking at Jack, no one could have guessed what lay ahead for them. He was completely relaxed. Apparently the seductive pulse of the city had already gotten to him. Placing his arm around her shoulders, he gazed at the young desk clerk and said, ''My wife and I are hoping that she'll be pregnant by the time we leave here in two days.'' Then he gazed down at Beth with a mischievous grin on his face. ''We're anxious to get started with our family, aren't we, dear?'' he added, giving her shoulders a light, playful-like squeeze.

Anxious, indeed, Beth thought.

The young desk clerk giggled even more than she had when she had learned they were newlyweds. "You know what?" she said. "I'm gonna give y'all the honeymoon suite. Y'all are lucky, too. It's usually booked."

She quickly jotted something down next to their names and then looked up at them and smiled. "It's said that every bride who has ever entered that suite with her groom on their wedding night has left it the following morning pregnant with her first child," the young woman boldly stated, obviously very pleased with herself for having imparted that bit of information to them.

"You don't say," Jack replied in awe.

A shiver passed down Beth's spine. She just hoped that she would turn out to be that lucky.

The clerk bent down under the desk and then came back into view a second later with a room key that she gave to the bellman who was waiting nearby. Then she bestowed Jack and Beth with an all-knowing grin. "Just follow Bains upstairs. He'll show y'all to your room."

The honeymoon suite turned out to be one of the most romantic bedrooms Beth had ever seen. It was all ruffles and lace of antique white and country blue with a hint of rose every now and then for added color. It had a high canopy over the bed and mosquito netting that was held back at all sides. Obviously the mosquito netting wasn't necessary. It was there for effect.

Their linens were made of one hundred percent bleached cotton, and someone had starched, ironed and then carefully folded each one. The pillowcases were trimmed in Battenburg Lace, as was the top sheet, Beth soon realized, after checking it out for herself.

The bathroom had a footed tub with a shelf overhead that was well stocked with old-time fragrances like lilac, honeysuckle and gardenia soaps. Large paintings of magnolias and one of a Live Oak tree garden hung on the walls. To Beth, it was a suite created for making babies. She had no idea how she and Jack had ended up staying here for their honeymoon, but she was very glad that they had.

"I'll get some ice and chill our last bottle of champagne," Jack said.

"I think I'd like to take a nice, leisurely bath," Beth replied, eyeing the bathroom one final time before turning back into the bedroom where he stood.

"I'll pin your hair up for you," he said.

"But I thought you were going downstairs for ice," she replied, giving him a surprised glance.

"I'm going, only I'll pin up your hair first."

When they had been kids, Jack used to comb her long hair all the time, but somewhere along their journey to adulthood, she had cut her hair shorter and he had stopped brushing it so often. In fact, she couldn't remember the last time he had. Years, probably. Surprisingly, it pleased Beth a great deal to know that he was still interested in her hair. She got the combs she always used when bathing from her suitcase and handed them to him. Then she sat down on a stool and watched his reflection in the mirror in front of her as he carefully pinned each strand of her hair in place on top of her head. She couldn't help but notice how straight and tall he was. How handsome…and sexy, too. Where had she been all these years? He was really a hunk. And now that she was giving it serious thought, he easily put the likes of Franko Malone to shame.

Finally Jack finished his task. But before letting her up from the stool, he placed his hands on her shoulders, bent down and kissed her lightly on the back of the neck.

"Thank you, Jack," she said, inspecting her new hairdo in the mirror in front of her. Her stomach quivered at the tantalizing feel of his lips on her neck. He looked up and their eyes met. If ever Beth had any concerns about his ability as her best friend to make love to her when the time finally came, they quickly dissolved into nothing. Suddenly she no longer had any doubts as to which one of them would have the courage to make the first move. To be sure, in his own way Jack had just let her know that he was already in the driver's seat. She was simply his passenger, going along for the ride.

Which, of course, was just fine with her. He was a lot better at this than she was anyway.

"I'll be right back," he said in that deep, coffee-rich voice of his.

Beth's pulse points throbbed as she watched him turn and walk out the door, closing it behind him.

Even after he was gone, it took her several moments to gather her equilibrium. Finally she stood, walked into the bathroom and turned on the water in the tub. She went to her suitcase and found the short silk alabaster white gown and matching robe set that Karen had talked her into buying a couple of days ago for her wedding night.

Well, no doubt about it, this was her wedding night.

She returned to the bathroom, found a decorative jar of foaming bath crystals on the shelf above the tub and poured a generous amount into the flowing water. An accumulation of lush bubbles gathered rather quickly at the foot of the tub, and the smell of gardenias filled the air. Shedding her clothes, Beth stepped into the warm water and slipped down beneath the bubbles floating on top until her body was completely submerged.

Minutes passed, and then she heard when Jack returned to their suite. A few moments later, the bathroom door opened and he entered, carrying two stemmed glasses. ''Chilled champagne. Compliments of the house,'' he said, walking over to where she was and handing her a glass. ''I went ahead and chilled the bottle we brought with us for later tonight,'' he added.

Without rising from beneath the thick layer of foamy bubbles that covered her naked body, Beth took a sip from her glass of champagne, then laid her head back on the rim of the tub. A few strands of her dark hair had come loose and now clung against the wet bare skin on the back of her neck. A light bead of perspiration dotted her forehead. The atmosphere in the small room was soft...cozy...alluring. "Mmm..." she groaned, deep and throaty. "This is the life, isn't it?"

Suddenly Jack plucked the glass she held from her fingers and placed it alongside his on a wooden stool nearby. Her eyes popped open at the abruptness of it all, and she saw that he had already removed his jacket. Now he was rolling up the sleeves of his shirt.

"W-what are you doing?" she asked, her heart beginning to pick up tempo.

Kneeling down at the side of the tub where she lay so helplessly naked beneath a mere layer of soapy bubbles, he grinned. "I'm going to give you a bath," he said.

The very idea of him doing such a thing was so sensual in nature that it sent an enormous heat surging through her body. The warm water she lay in...the soapy foam surrounding her...the heavy fragrance of gardenias...the chilled champagne she'd drunk...the thin layer of steam on the bathroom mirror—they all mingled together now to give her a light, heady sensation.

He picked up the bar of soap she had chosen for herself only moments ago and began to make a thick lather in the palms of his hands. Finally he said, "Sit up, Beth, so I can soap your back."

But that meant exposing her breasts, too, right?

Beth gave it only a moment's thought and then sat up. Soap bubbles slid down into her cleavage and over the mounds of her breasts. She looked up at Jack to see what he was doing and found he was watching the soap slide and grinning. But there was a certain light in his eyes and Beth had a feeling she knew exactly where that light was going to eventually lead them. There was no turning back now. But then, she didn't really want to anymore. This was all part of her plan.

His hands were slick, soapy, and doing wonderful things to the tense muscles in her shoulders and neck. He worked his thumbs up and down and in small circles, and it was driving her completely over the edge. Beth closed her eyes to savor the moment. She was beginning to think she'd died and gone to heaven and hated the thought of ever having to open her eyes again.

But then his hands slipped over her shoulders and down to her breasts, and he gave them the same tender, loving massage that he'd given the muscles in her neck and shoulders. Beth thought surely that the pleasure was going to be more than she could bear. Frankly she didn't think life in that moment could have possibly gotten any better.

But soon, it was all to clear that she was wrong. It did get better—and quickly. The moment his hands slipped farther down her body and found the pivotal point of her womanhood, her whole world exploded into a million—zillion—sparkling pieces. "Oh, Jack," she moaned. "I think you'd better stop now."

"Beth, honey," he drawled, leaning in close enough to kiss the side of her face, "I'm just getting started."

In the next moment he lifted her out of the bathtub as though she weighed less than a feather, carried her back into the most romantic bedroom she'd ever been in and placed her wet-soaked body across the softest bed she'd ever slept on.

"Jack, what are you doing?" she asked. Her breath caught in her throat when he gazed down at her in a way that told her exactly what he was planning to do.

Within seconds, he stripped off his clothes and was completely naked. Then, with his hands on his hips and that heated look still on his face, he said, "Beth, don't you think it's time you stopped asking so many questions?"

A moment later Beth watched in awe as he lowered himself on top of her.

"But, Jack..." she said, her breath stalling at the feel of his naked skin suddenly pressed against her naked skin. Her heart began to pound.

He took her lips in one long, leisurely kiss. When finally he ended it, he looked deep into her eyes. "What do you want to ask me, Beth?"

"I...I...uh...just wanted to know one thing. I—is this just going to be foreplay between us right now? Or are you planning for us to go all the way with this?"

"You want a baby, don't you?" he asked, as though she needed to be reminded of that fact. But, of course, she didn't.

"Yes."

"Then what do you think?"

"I...uh...I think we're going to go all the way."

"I think you're right," he answered.

And then her best friend claimed her lips again, only this time even more passionately, driving her need to have him to the point of desperation. His hands worked their magic on her, and with his strong body he gave her what she wanted most from him. He gave her a chance at being pregnant with the child she had always wanted.

"Thank you, Jack," she whispered later that night, right before dozing off in his arms for what seemed like the twentieth time. He'd already awakened her so many times that night to make love to her that she was exhausted from the sweet agony of it all.

He tightened his arms around her and kissed her lightly on the temple. "My pleasure," he drawled in a voice so deep, so rich with passion that even with her body completely sated, chills shimmied down her spine. He settled himself comfortably beside her, and soon they both fell into a deep, exhausted slumber.

Chapter Nine

When Beth woke up the following morning, she was alone in bed. Her first thought was that she was starving.

She heard the water running in the bathroom and instantly knew where to find her husband. He was taking a shower.

Still naked under the covers, she yawned, stretched and thought about the night before and all that she and Jack had done together. She had never in a million years thought that having sex with her best friend would have been so…so powerful. So all-consuming. Frankly if she wasn't already pregnant by now, she needed to see a doctor. Something was terribly wrong with her.

Of course, she was going to have to wait at least a couple of weeks before finding out for sure. She had her fingers crossed, though.

But in the meantime she wasn't planning to waste a single day of being married to Jack. There weren't any guarantees that his seed had already taken in her. Therefore, it was her purpose—if not her duty—to have sex with him at every single opportunity presented her.

Right?

Right.

And to her way of thinking, right this very moment was as good an opportunity as any.

First of all, they were alone.

Secondly, it was their honeymoon.

And, of course, Jack would know exactly why she was doing it. He had in mind to accomplish the very same mission.

Boldly throwing back the covers on the bed, she slipped her feet down to the floor and trotted quietly to the door of the bathroom. Without making a sound, she pressed her ear against it and listened to hear if Jack was indeed still in the shower. It sounded as though he was.

She turned the knob and the door opened, so she stuck her head inside. Sure enough, he was in the small shower stall at one corner of the bathroom. The whole room was steamed up from the hot water pouring down on him.

Beth slipped her entire body inside the room and tiptoed to the shower. Then, suddenly, she drew back the shower curtain. Taken by total surprise, Jack whirled around to face her. "Hey, what are you doing?'' he asked when a second later she stepped right into the narrow shower stall with him.

Placing her hands on her hips, Beth gazed up at him with an exasperated look on her face. ''Jack,'' she said, ''don't you think it's time you stopped asking so many questions?''

It took him a moment, but finally a grin eased across his face. ''You're damned right, it is,'' he said.

Then he pulled the shower curtain closed, and Beth got her first lesson in making love to her husband in a small, damp, cramped space.

As it turned out, Jack made it into quite a memorable occasion for her. One she wasn't likely to ever forget. Nor did she want to.

By noon that day, they both decided that they couldn't tolerate their hunger pangs any longer and voted unanimously to go out for food. They dressed and then wandered along Decatur Street until they found a small sidewalk café that appealed to them. For the next couple of hours they sat and ate overstuffed Po-boys and drank iced tea, and watched the continuous stream of tourists that flocked by them.

They spent the remainder of the afternoon doing that same scene. They walked along the banks of the Mississippi River, bought a painting Beth liked from a gallery on Royal Street and then gave encouragement to a beginning artist who was displaying his work along Jackson Square. They spent a quiet moment inside St. Louis Cathedral, shared a Hurricane at Pat O'Brien's Bar on St. Peter Street and then did some shopping at the Riverwalk. Beth bought herself a pair of shoes. Jack bought himself a baseball cap. On their way back to their hotel, they stopped at the Café du Monde Coffee Stand in the French Market for beignets and coffee.

Beth's feet were hurting by the time they got back to their hotel, so Jack offered to give them a massage. In turn, she gave him the back rub he requested—in the nude, of course. It was the way he wanted it. But in the end, he turned over flat on his back in bed and gave her a thorough massage instead. Now, it seemed, just giving him a good, old-fashioned back rub was never going to be the same again.

Beth went into the bathroom for a while and when she came out she was mildly surprised to find that Jack had fallen asleep on the bed. Actually she was kind of glad that he had. She needed a rest herself. She climbed in next to him and snuggled close.

It was such a comforting thought to know that her best friend was only a whisper, a touch, away. It made everything she was doing to accomplish her dream in life seem sane, when in fact she knew that it really wasn't. But that was the special quality about Jack... about their friendship. It made sense when nothing else in her life did.

Like this honeymoon.

It was so out of control, it was ridiculous.

Just how many times had they already made love? She'd lost count!

Now wasn't that plum ridiculous of someone who was always able to keep track of everything else that happened to her in life?

Well, of course, it was. Only…

Only she was with Jack, so that made it okay. And because of that one single factor, she firmly believed that she, too, was going to be okay. And when this was all over with, she would have her baby.

She was certain of it. Jack's baby.

She knew he didn't want her thinking that way, and she'd promised him—and herself, too—that she wouldn't. She planned to keep that promise. She just liked to sneak that thought in every once in a while. It made her feel all warm inside.

It was no big deal, really. Nothing for either of them to worry about. She was the last person who was going to get sentimental over what they were doing together. She knew what kind of trouble that could lead to. Jack was doing her a big favor. They both knew this marriage was nothing more than a business deal between two good friends. No more. No less. It was the way she had wanted it from the very beginning, and it was still the one, single guarantee she had that their friendship was going to survive all of this.

Minutes passed. Needing something to do, Beth studied the features of Jack's face. After all, they had been friends for so long that there were a lot of things about him she had begun to take for granted. Soon, however, she grew even more restless and pulled a feather out from the pillow beneath his head. She began to tease him awake by dragging it lightly across the bridge of his nose.

He didn't actually come awake. He just groaned and then moved slightly to one side.

She grinned. This was going to be fun.

She caressed him with the feather again, only this time across his lips.

He twitched his mouth in response.

She got brave and straddled him. Leaning down into his face, she kissed him until he began to come awake.

All of him.

Wide-awake.

And hard.

It now looked as though they were gong to make love again. So much for tickling him awake with a feather…

Actually this kind of behavior was getting to be quite a habit for them. A habit that, sooner or later, Beth knew, they were going to have to break.

But she didn't want to think about that right now. She just wanted to think about what a pleasurable time she and Jack were having, trying to get her pregnant. She had never dreamed it would be like this.

Of course, she had always known that he was the right man for the job. She had only to convince him of that fact.

Well, it looked as though he was now convinced.

Jack was now doing deliciously wicked things to her body, and soon Beth lost track of all rational thinking. She groaned and moaned and pleaded and begged, while Jack took her time after time and gave her exactly what she was asking for.

Eventually they had pizza delivered to their hotel suite because they both decided that they were too exhausted to go out to dinner.

But it was a blissful exhaustion and Beth couldn't have been more satisfied with the results of her plan thus far.

And to think, tomorrow was a whole other day that she was going to get to spend with Jack in their honeymoon suite.

Just how many more ways were there to make love anyway? she wondered.

She couldn't wait to find out.

Gone, it seemed, was the prudish young woman she had once been, she thought, as once again she lay in Jack's arms and slipped off into an exhausted sleep. She couldn't say it wasn't a fair trade-off.

Because without a doubt, she knew that it was.

That night they slept sound and didn't wake until the sun rose on the following morning. Because it was the last day of their honeymoon, they spent the entire time in bed making love. After all, they were on a mission to get her pregnant and, by golly, they were going to do their best to accomplish that task.

But finally, the day was coming to a close and they both knew it was time to pack up their belongings, rent a car and return home. On the two-hour drive back, they came to the conclusion that it would be more convenient for Jack to move into her place for the short duration of their marriage.

They arrived at her house just before midnight, unpacked their clothes and then made love in the shower one last time for the sake of…well…for the sake of getting her pregnant. They knew eventually it would all have to end, but that was still a couple of months down the road yet. There was plenty of time left for them to enjoy each other.

They were awakened the next morning when the telephone rang next to Beth's bed, and they both realized that they'd overslept the alarm they had set. Jumping out on each side of the bed, they made a mad scramble to get dressed for work.

Ironically they were ready to walk out of the house at the same time. In the garage, Jack suddenly trapped Beth against the front fender of her car. "I'm sorry about this morning," he said. "I'll try to find a way to make it up to you soon."

"What do you mean?" she asked, smiling at him. She thought it was kind of neat, their leaving at the same time like this to go to their jobs. This was probably how it was every weekday morning for most married couples in America. The husband went off to his job. The wife went off to hers. The kids, if there were any, went off to school or daycare. She liked the comforting I'll-have-dinner-cooked-for-you-tonight-honey kind of feeling it gave her. Jack was so handsome in his business suit. She was so proud he was her friend…her husband.

For the time being, at least, she was living her dream.

Unbidden, Beth thought of the way Jack made her feel when they were naked together in bed and her stomach quivered. His intense loving over the past couple of days had turned her completely inside out. Thanks to him, her soul was soaring somewhere in the clouds, and what was left of her down on earth felt a sense of freedom unlike anything she'd ever felt before. She felt whole, complete. And sometimes when she wasn't being very careful, she almost felt like a woman in love.

But, of course, she wasn't in love. Not with Jack, for heaven's sake. But then she wasn't supposed to be. Oh, she loved him, all right, she reminded herself. But there was a big difference in loving him her way and her being in love with him.

However, that didn't explain the way she felt when her soul was roaring up in the clouds somewhere. That was something that had never happened to her before, and she had always thought it was something that would happen only when she fell in love. Obviously she had been wrong. Just loving Jack as her closest friend was enough to make that happen for her.

And why shouldn't it? She and Jack were completely devoted to each other. They didn't need to be in love. They had something better going for them. Their friendship was as solid and dependable as a rock.

Jack moved in closer, almost as if he planned to whisper something in her ear. "I didn't do my job this morning," he said. "But I promise it won't happen again."

After kissing her on the mouth, he walked to his

car that had remained in her garage since their wedding day, got in and drove away.

Beth watched him go, her heart pounding in her throat. There was absolutely no doubt in her mind that he had every intention of keeping his promise.

And she found that she was counting on it.

Beth's telephone rang in her office for what seemed like the hundredth time that morning. She glanced at the clock on her desk. It was five minutes until noon. She glanced at her daily appointment calendar just to be sure that her lunch hour was free. It was. She had been so busy all morning, she needed the hour-long break. She picked up the receiver. "Hello."

"Beth, it's Jack. Got any plans for lunch?"

"Lunch... Gosh, I've been so busy trying to catch up this morning, I haven't even had time to think about lunch."

"Good. Then meet me at home in ten minutes," he said.

"Home? But I don't think I have anything to fix us for lunch at home."

"Don't worry about it. I'll pick up Chinese. Just be there, Beth. Okay?"

It was something in his tone of voice that enlightened Beth to the fact that it wasn't only lunch he was planning for them to share. Suddenly she was breathless. "All right, then. I'll be there."

He hung up, and Beth didn't waste any time gathering up her purse to leave from her office.

Less than fifteen minutes later, she arrived home.

Seconds later, Jack drove up right behind her. By the time she had fumbled with the key in the back door of her house and got it opened, he had walked up and was already beginning to pull the pins from her hair. Without saying a word, he told her exactly what he had in mind.

Beth could hardly wait.

Once they were inside the house, Jack immediately dropped the bag of Chinese food on the kitchen table, turned and pinned her to the spot with his gaze.

"This is insane, Jack," she said, breathless. "We're supposed to be just friends."

"I know," he said with a gleam in his eyes that said he couldn't have cared less about how insane this whole thing was. He wanted her.

She wanted him, too.

"I thought of you all morning long," he said gruffly.

"You're all I thought about, too," she confessed. "What are we going to do, Jack? I think we've crossed the line."

"No way," he said, shaking his head. "We're not over the line. Not yet."

"But how can you be so sure?" Beth asked.

Stopping short, he took a step back from her and held out his hands in a form of surrender. "Look, I could stop all of this in a moment, if I wanted to," he said. "Couldn't you?"

"W-well…yes, of course," Beth stammered, taken completely off guard by his question. "If I wanted to."

"Then, see," he said, "we aren't over any line yet."

"I'm not so sure, Jack," she said hesitantly.

"Well, I am," he replied.

Jack had already taken off his suit coat and tossed it carelessly across the countertop. Now he was pulling off his tie and unbuttoning his shirt.

Beth placed her purse down on the counter next to his suit coat and then slipped her feet out of her pumps. She had made her decision. For the moment, at least, she chose to believe him.

"Hungry?" he asked with a sexy, lopsided grin on his face as he backed her toward her bedroom.

"Starving," she replied. Every cell in her body tingled with anticipation.

Suddenly the gleam in his eyes intensified. "Turn around," he commanded. "I'll unzip your dress."

She did. The next thing she knew, her dress was lying at her feet.

He spun her around and kissed her hard on the mouth, and she found she wanted him so badly in that moment, she thought she would explode.

Somehow they made it to her bed, and he took her…quickly…hungrily. They both knew they didn't have much time for what they were doing. All the same she had wanted it fast and furious. And, of course, Jack, as always, had been more than willing to accommodate her needs.

Afterward, having little time to linger together in bed, they got dressed, shared lunch and arrived back at their jobs without a minute to spare.

At five o'clock, Beth found herself anxious to get home again to be with Jack…to hold him…to make love with him. A part of her was wondering just where all of this was leading her—leading them—but for now she didn't want to think about it.

In spite of her efforts to protect herself from disappointment, her world came crashing down around her when Jack returned home later that night. She saw the deep lines in his forehead and knew that something was wrong.

"I've got bad news," he said. "It's my job. Malone got demoted today, so that means I'm going to take his place and travel overseas sooner than I expected. In fact, I have to leave tomorrow, and I'll be gone for at least two weeks."

"Two weeks?" Beth exclaimed, her heart sinking. "That's a long time."

"I know," he said, pulling her into his arms the moment he saw tears in her eyes. "But I don't have a choice. I've got to go."

Beth nodded. It was his job, after all. Of course, he had to go. It was just that she didn't want him to.

"Maybe this trip is for the best," he said. "After all, we need to keep perspective on things. We never planned for this to go on forever, and I think we both need to remember that."

He was right, of course. She of all people wasn't going to disagree with him on that one.

Suddenly Jack lifted her chin so that she had to look him in the eyes. "Beth, I want you to promise me something. If you should even suspect that you're pregnant while I'm gone, please don't do anything to find out for sure until I get back."

"Oh, Jack, I promise I won't," she said, burying her face against his chest and wishing with all her heart that she could go with him. Right now, two weeks apart seemed like an eternity to her. But she couldn't just pick up and leave. She had her agency to consider. Still, this was such a critical time in her life. She needed him here with her.

Their lovemaking that night was fierce and passionate, urgent and greedy. It was as though they were trying to save up enough satisfaction to last them while they were apart.

The following day Beth drove Jack to the airport. She kissed him goodbye at the gate, and somehow, through it all, was miraculously able to hold back her emotions until he was on board his flight. But the moment she saw his plane moving toward takeoff, she leaned her forehead against the glass wall in front of her and let the tears roll down her face.

She was missing him terribly already.

Somehow, she made it through the next couple of weeks. Jack called her often during that time. He told her that he missed her and was anxious to come home. She told him she was counting the days. She missed him and couldn't wait for him to get back.

One morning, she realized her period was late. Never in her life was her period late. Normally she was like clockwork. Almost to the hour.

She was exuberantly happy at the possibility of being pregnant. Spellbound, even. And her first thought was that she couldn't wait to tell Jack.

Oh, God, Jack… If she was pregnant, then that meant—

She couldn't bear to think about what that meant. Not right now, anyway. She was missing him too much.

Jack called her that night from London and told her he would be home the following evening. The next day turned out to be one of the longest days of Beth's life. The only place she ventured was the neighborhood supermarket, and then she came straight home to wait for him. She didn't want to chance that he might get in earlier than expected.

But by nightfall, he still hadn't arrived, and Beth was on pins and needles waiting for him. Finally, near midnight, she heard a cab drive up to the curb in front of her house. Before the driver could even get out from behind the wheel and unload Jack's luggage from the trunk, she was already running down the sidewalk to meet Jack. Reaching him, she practically threw herself in his arms.

Jack hugged her tight against him. ''God, I missed you,'' he said, kissing her on the mouth.

''I missed you, too,'' she replied breathlessly. It was such a comforting thought to know that he was finally home.

He picked up his luggage and they went inside the house together. Beth closed the door behind them. Then, taking him by the hand, she immediately began leading him down the hall toward her bedroom.

"What's this?" he said with a teasing grin.

"Your homecoming present," she replied.

He didn't say a word, just grinned and followed her lead.

Once they reached her bedroom, they helped each other to disrobe and then made love with such an intensity that it almost made up for their two weeks of lost time. Over and over again, he took her lips, her body, her heart and her soul and made them his.

When the fire between them was sated, Beth knew that she had something of critical importance to tell him and that putting it off, even for a moment, wasn't going to change anything. That something was the source of the most painful, bittersweet joy she had ever known. Just thinking about it now made her want to cry. Only she couldn't cry. Too much was at stake.

"Jack," she said softly, moving her head slightly until she was able to look at him. Unconsciously she placed the palm of her hand against his bare chest and stroked him lovingly.

He was lying flat on his back with his eyes closed. "Hum?" he said without moving a muscle.

"I have something I need to tell you."

"I was kind of wondering when you were going to get around to that," he said.

"How did you know I had something on my mind?"

"Because I know you, Beth."

"I think I'm pregnant, Jack."

There was a moment of dead silence where Beth was almost certain she could hear her own heartbeat.

Finally he said, "Well, that's good, isn't it?"

"Yeah—it's great."

"You must be very happy," he replied.

"Oh, I am."

"Then I'm happy for you," he said.

But the fact of the matter was, he didn't look very happy. Not to Beth, anyway. As far as she could tell, he hadn't moved one single muscle of his body since she'd started this conversation with him. True, he had opened his eyes, but he was staring straight up at the ceiling.

"W-well, actually," she stammered, "I don't know for sure if I'm really pregnant. I mean, I haven't taken a pregnancy test or anything. I bought one today, but I...uh...I was waiting for you to get back before taking it. Remember, you said you wanted me to wait for you to be here when I did?"

"I remember," he said, but his voice was still lacking any real enthusiasm. She wished he would smile, or something. Anything, in fact, was better than the stone-faced reaction she was getting from him right now. Didn't he have any idea what it was doing to her?

She frowned. "Jack, is there something wrong?" she asked, lifting her head slightly and gazing at him.

"No," he said. "Nothing's wrong. I guess I just wasn't expecting you to get pregnant this soon, that's all."

"Well, I wasn't expecting it to happen this soon, either. But it only takes one little, bitty sperm," she said laughingly, hoping to make him smile. All she wanted was for him to smile. Or say something to make her feel better. She needed him so much right now. Why couldn't he see that?

But he didn't smile. In fact, he didn't say anything at all. Suddenly Beth found herself fighting back a wave of tears. But she wouldn't let him see her cry. Not one single tear. She had some pride, after all.

She swallowed back the lump in her throat. "Jack, I'd really like to take the pregnancy test tonight, before we go to sleep, if it's all right with you."

"But it's not up to me, Beth," he said. "It's up to you. You're the one calling the shots, remember?"

She frowned at his remark. She wasn't trying to call the shots. She was just trying to get him to tell her what was bothering him.

Taking a deep breath, she swung her feet to the floor and sat up. "Aren't you happy for me?" she said, giving him a long, thoughtful glance.

He tucked his hands behind his head and continued to stare up at the ceiling as though she weren't even there. "If this is what you want, I am."

She shrugged. "Well, of course, it's what I want. Having my own baby is what I've always wanted." After standing up, she gazed down at him. "Look, I know you're tired and all, but I have one more favor to ask of you."

After what seemed like an eternity, he cut his piercing eyes in her direction.

Beth got a sick feeling in the pit of her stomach, but she was determined not to let it stop her from going ahead with the moment. "I'd like for you to be there when I take the pregnancy test. You know, when the color changes and all. According to the directions on the box, it doesn't take that long for it to happen.''

After a long, drawn-out silence that did absolutely nothing to make her stomach feel any better, Jack sighed heavily. ''Yeah, sure, why not,'' he said. Then he swung his legs to the floor and in one fluid motion stood up.

Standing there naked next to him, Beth felt suddenly very vulnerable. Immediately she reached for her robe and slipped it on.

She didn't understand why she felt the way she did, but she knew she needed to be on guard where her feelings were concerned.

And the most devastating part of it all was knowing that she had to be on guard with the one person in all the world whom she would have willingly trusted with her life.

Chapter Ten

*P*regnant!

The color code said Beth was pregnant.

Jack's gut knotted. He couldn't believe this was happening to him. Not already. He and Beth had only been together—what? two weeks. It was too soon. He had been counting on having more time with her. Damn, what luck. She was already pregnant.

"We'll have to decide on what attorney to use for our divorce," she said.

"W-what…?" Jack replied, immediately trying to pull his thoughts together. Here he was thinking of how much he was going to miss not being intimate with her any longer and here she was already planning their divorce. These past two weeks hadn't caused her to budge one inch in her ideas about them. They were going to have a baby together, but even that hadn't changed her mind. And he was fool enough to think that maybe it would. She loved him, all right, but only as a friend.

Suck in your pride, Kincaid, he told himself. You're not her Knight in Shining Armor, and you never will be. Instead, you hold the coveted title of being her best friend. And according to Beth's way of thinking, those two roles in her life simply didn't mesh. It was one or the other. He should be happy he got something.

Besides, he reminded himself, he didn't really want to be married and have a kid on the way. He was a bachelor by nature. He would not be happy for very long being anything else. He was just feeling a bit shaken right now. Beth had a way of doing that to him.

"Look," he said, turning away from the test results that told him his way of life for the past two weeks was now coming to a quick close, "I'm tired. I don't want to talk about finding an attorney tonight. Let's just go to bed and get some sleep."

"All right," Beth said.

Jack could tell by the expression on her face that she wasn't all that sure how to take his lack of response. But in spite of that, she led the way as they returned to bed. After turning off the lamp next to her, she lay back against the mattress and said, "Jack, are you feeling okay?"

"I'm fine, Beth. I'm just tired," he replied.

"Well, you certainly have all the reason in the

world to be," she said. "Hopefully you'll feel better in the morning."

"I'm sure, I will," he said. "Good night."

"Good night."

At that point, Jack had every intention of rolling over to his side of the mattress and going right to sleep, but then he thought about the limited time he now had in her bed—in her arms—and pulled Beth close to him instead. They fell asleep curled up together.

Beth rose the next day, which was Sunday, around midmorning. But since Jack was still in such a deep sleep, she simply closed the door to her bedroom without disturbing him and went into the kitchen to make a pot of coffee.

Besides, she had a lot to think about and needed some time to herself.

She was pregnant! She could hardly believe it. It should have been the most wonderful feeling in the world—and it was. It was just that…well, there was a touch of sadness, too, and she had no idea where it had come from. Frankly it wasn't part of her plan.

In and out. Short and quick. No time for her and Jack to fall in love. That was the way she had organized this whole thing and, by golly, she was sticking to her plan. To falter now would undoubtedly prove to be a big mistake at some future date. Already there were times when she sensed an unexplainable tenseness between her and Jack. A tenseness that was sending off warning bells she could no longer allow herself to ignore. Now that she was pregnant, it was time to end their marriage as soon as possible so that their lives could return to normal.

Jack slept late into the afternoon. When he finally got up, he showered, ate a light supper and watched television for a while. At eight-thirty that night, he said he was going back to bed. By now Beth knew for certain that something was bothering him, something that had to do with her pregnancy test coming out positive, because his manner with her had changed too suddenly after that. Beth thought she knew exactly what it was. Now that he'd gotten her pregnant as she wanted, he was ready for her to keep her end of the bargain. He was ready to have his freedom back.

Well, he deserved it. It was the least she could do for him after what he'd just done for her.

So why then, was a part of her being so resistant to the idea of getting a divorce from him when it had been such an intricate part of her plan all along?

She was just being greedy, she told herself a moment later. And that, she knew, was no way to handle a friendship that she cherished more than anything in the world. Jack deserved to have his freedom back without having to ask her for it. He was her dearest friend, and she loved him too much to place him under that kind of pressure. Therefore, she was going to see to it that she gave him what he wanted. In fact, she planned to take care of it first thing in the morning.

Beth went to bed after the late-night news, and was

surprised to discover that Jack was still awake. He rolled over suddenly and reached for her. And although he made no attempt to explain his reserved behavior from earlier that night, she gladly went into his arms and let him make love to her. After all, he was her husband…her lover…her best friend…her world. They made love twice that night before finally going to sleep.

The following morning, after being awakened by the alarm, Jack never once brought up the subject of her being pregnant, or the fact that he was dying to have his freedom back. But then, he really didn't have to. She knew that he was. Still, when he reached for her again and their eyes met, she surrendered herself to him—her body, her soul—with complete abandonment. Because she knew this was it. By that night, they would be officially separated. And these were the last, stolen, bittersweet moments they would ever have together like this.

Jack stood behind his desk after eight long hours at work and gazed down at the new ad campaign for his company that he held in his hands. It wasn't complete yet—not by a long shot—but he liked it already. He thought his boss would, too.

He was just glad that something was going right today, because to be honest his personal life was in shambles. Now that Beth was pregnant, she had made it quite clear to him that she was no longer in need of his services as her sperm donor and was getting ready to divorce him. He should have been happy about that, but he wasn't. Instead he was miserable.

The truth was, he was over the line. He was in love with her.

Actually he now realized that he'd always been in love with her. It had just taken the last two weeks of his life for him to come to recognize that.

Suddenly his secretary buzzed him.

"What is it, Pam?" he asked.

"It's Beth on line three."

His gut knotted. "Thanks."

He pressed down the button to line three. "Hello."

"Jack, it's Beth. Look, I'm at the office of Jerome Hyatt. He's the attorney I've just hired to get our divorce proceedings started. He just needs to know—"

"You're where?" he cut in as all air rushed from his lungs.

There was a long, startled pause. Finally Beth said, "I-I'm at the office of our attorney. You know, the one I told you I was going to hire to file the necessary papers to get our divorce started."

Jack gaped into the telephone. He couldn't believe this was happening. "Already?" he remarked, his heart pounding in his throat.

"W-well, Jack, I'm pregnant. What's the point of putting it off?" Beth asked.

The point?

The point was, he was her husband, dammit. The father of her child. She couldn't just use him to get pregnant and then discard him like this. He had his rights, too. She wasn't getting rid of him that easily.

And frankly he'd had enough of it. For as long as he could remember, he had allowed Beth to call the shots concerning their friendship because he had feared he would lose her altogether if he didn't. Well, now it was his turn to decide the way things needed to be, and his first order of business was to confront the emotional stuff going on between them. He was tired of having to lie to himself when it came to his feelings for her. Beth probably wouldn't want to hear what he had to say, but one way or another he was going to make her listen. Then, if she still didn't want him as her husband, he would have to learn to live with that. But, at least, he would have been honest with her—and with himself, too. At this point in the game, it was probably his only chance of convincing her of anything. Besides, he owed that much to their baby.

His baby. That was something else he and Beth had to straighten out. None of this *best friend* business anymore. He was the kid's father, and that was the role he was going to play in his kid's life. Of course, he wasn't planning to use his paternity as leverage in convincing Beth that they belonged together—except, of course, if he really needed to. He was at a point where he wasn't above resorting to blackmail.

"Beth," he said, keeping his voice calm, "don't you dare sign any papers until I get there."

"B-but, Jack, it isn't necessary that you come."

"Like hell, it isn't. This is my life, too, you know," he replied.

He hung up the telephone before she could reply, then quickly looked up the address of the attorney she'd named and stormed out of his office. When he arrived at his destination, he was told by the secretary at the front desk that Mr. Hyatt and Mrs. Kincaid were expecting him.

As Jack entered the attorney's office, Jerome Hyatt immediately rose from his seat and introduced himself. Then he invited Jack to have a seat in the chair next to Beth.

But Jack hadn't come to sit back and listen to anyone make long-winded speeches about the laws of divorce in the state of Louisiana. He had come to talk to his wife, and that was exactly what he was going to do.

Gazing at Beth, but directing his words to her attorney, Jack placed his hands on his hips and said, "Look, I know this is going to seem like a strange request to you, Hyatt—especially under the circumstances—but, you see, there seems to have been a misunderstanding between my wife and me, so I need to speak to her alone for a moment." Jack canvassed the room, looking for an outlet. "Is there someplace where she and I can talk in private?"

"Uh…well…yes," the attorney said, obviously flustered by Jack's request. "That door over there leads into my private rest room. But, look here, I don't want any trouble."

"There won't be any trouble," Jack said, shaking

his head. "Didn't my wife explain? She and I have been the best of friends practically all our lives. In fact, that's the reason we're supposedly getting this divorce. We want to stay friends," he said with just a hint of sarcasm.

"I see," the attorney said, his eyes growing round. He cleared his throat nervously and sat down behind his desk.

Jack turned his eyes back to Beth. "Shall we?" he said, motioning with his head toward the rest room door.

"Jack…" Beth replied hesitantly, as he walked forward and took her by the arm. "What's this all about?"

"We'll talk," he said. "In private."

Beth had to practically run to keep up with his quick pace. She looked back at the attorney and tried to smile as though there was nothing out of the ordinary going on. But she could tell by the look on the man's face that he was completely flabbergasted. She could only imagine that not too many of his clients— if any, at all—had ever asked to use his private rest room as their conference chamber.

And then she thought of some of the other faux pas she and Jack had pulled together over the years and grimaced. Leave it to them to find a way to make a spectacle of themselves, even when filing for a divorce they both wanted.

Beth was astounded by Jack's aggressive, if not oppressive, behavior. She was having enough trouble trying to keep her own emotions out of the way of what she was doing. Was it really necessary for him to come along like this and drag her off to some closet-size men's room to tell her what was on his mind when she already knew it was his freedom he was after?

They were at the rest room door within seconds. Jack stepped inside first, pulling Beth right along behind him. Then Jack shut the door and placed his hands on his hips.

"What? What is it?" she asked, gazing up at him in confusion. After all, she was doing this for him— for them—for their friendship. Why, she wondered, was he looking at her as if she had just slapped him across the face?

"What do you think you're doing?" he asked, his eyes boring heatedly into hers.

"W-what do you mean, what am I doing?" Beth stammered, her pulses racing to an all-time high. "I-I'm starting our divorce proceedings. Don't you want me to?"

Jack unconsciously ran his fingers through his hair. "Well, yes, of course, I do, only—"

Suddenly he realized what he was saying—what he had always said over the years in order to make it sound as though he was in complete agreement with anything she had to say concerning their friendship— and stopped himself point-blank. Taking her by the shoulders, he gazed deep into her eyes. "No, Beth. Frankly, I don't want you to start the divorce proceedings."

"Well, actually," she said, swallowing back the

sudden lump in her throat, "I thought of putting it off for a while, too, but then I decided that wouldn't be fair to you."

"To me?" Jack said incredulously.

Holding back a sudden rush of tears, Beth nodded. Because in that moment she made a startling discovery about herself. Somehow, at some point in all of this, she crossed the line she'd drawn to protect herself—to protect her friendship with Jack—and now she was in love with him. It was a terrifying realization, and it left her trembling inside. "You held up your end of our bargain, Jack, so now I need to hold up mine. You deserve to have your freedom back, and I'm just trying to give it to you."

"You're doing this for me?" Jack asked, drawing his eyebrows together in disbelief.

"And for our friendship. I need you so much, Jack. You were right, you know," she said, her eyes now filling with tears in spite of herself. "You are my Knight in Shining Armor in all the ways that really count. But regardless of my feelings, I can't suffocate your needs. I know you don't want to be married and have a child. And I know if I tried to force that on you now, it would ruin everything for us. I need you in my life too much for that."

Jack sucked in a deep breath. Suddenly he saw the whole picture, and his heartbeat kicked into high gear. For heaven's sake, Beth was in love with him, too. There shouldn't have been any problem between them. Only there was, thanks to Beth's diehard feelings about their remaining just good friends. How could he convince her that her dream of marriage and children had somehow become his dream, too? But he couldn't do it here, not in this attorney's office. He had to get her somewhere to himself. Somewhere he could remind her of just how good they were together. And not just as friends, but as lovers, too.

"Come on," he said a second later, taking her hand into his. "We have some serious communicating to do. But what I have in mind can't be done here."

"Where are we going?" she asked in bewilderment.

"Home," he replied, his eyes penetrating hers.

Fresh tears gathered in Beth's eyes. "Oh, Jack," she cried, "I'm so sorry I did this to us. We were perfectly happy when we were just friends. But then I had to go and mess everything up by asking you to be the father of my child. Now everything is ruined, and it's all my fault."

"It's not ruined, Beth," he said, suddenly taking her by the shoulders. "We're in love, for crying out loud. It's not the end of the world. It can be just the beginning for us. I'm telling you, baby, we're good together. We're good friends…and we're good at being lovers, too. Most couples I know would give anything to have what we do. We can make it, Beth, you and me. But you have to give us that chance."

"You love me?"

"Of course," he replied. "Can't you see that?"

By now hot, burning tears were rolling down Beth's face. "It's not that I want to end all this, because deep down inside, I know I don't. But I'm

afraid that if I don't, in the end I'll lose you altogether. And that would be terrible, Jack.''

Jack gently wiped at her tears with the tips of his
fingers. Then he lifted her face and made her look at
him. ''Beth, honey, don't you see? You don't ever
have to worry about that. Look, we've been through
a lot together already, and you haven't lost me yet.
I'm not going anywhere. Not without my best friend
at my side. Give us a chance, Beth. There aren't any
guarantees in life, but I can tell you this much. These
last two weeks have been a real eye-opener for me. I
want the baby we've made together, and I want you.
I promise, I will spend the rest of my days loving
you, loving our baby, every bit as much as I do right
now. But you've got to trust me on this one, Beth.
That's all I can say.''

It was enough, considering the source was Jack. He
was, after all, her most trustworthy friend. She believed in him as she believed in no other.

Making a sudden decision, one she had once fought
so hard for so long against, Beth took a deep, decisive
breath. ''I've fallen madly, head over heels in love
with you, Jack,'' she said, her eyes growing big and
round and somewhat frightened of what she was saying. And yet she had to say it, because it was true.
''So deeply, in fact, that sometimes it almost scares
me.''

He pulled her into his arms and crushed her against
his chest. ''I know,'' he said gruffly. ''Sometimes the
way I feel about you scares me, too.''

She pulled back suddenly and gazed at him. ''But

what if we blow it like my parents did and ruin everything?'' she asked.

"But what if we don't?'' he said, gazing deep into her eyes. "The way I see it, we've already been in love for a long time now, and we haven't blown it yet. Besides, this is not your parents' life, Beth. It's yours. It's up to you to live it like you want.''

Jack was right, and she knew it. When it came to knowing what was best for her, he was always right. He was as dependable as the rising sun.

She looked up and their eyes met. And then she knew for sure. He was, in fact, her rising sun.

He was her everything.

She smiled at him with complete trust.

He grinned back.

Then he opened the door to the rest room and they stepped out. Their attorney was waiting. Sitting up straight in his chair, he cleared his throat. "Well then,'' he said, "now that you've had your little talk, shall we proceed with the divorce?''

"Well, actually,'' Jack said, scooping up Beth's purse from the chair where she'd left it, "my wife and I have talked it over, and we've decided that a divorce is not the answer for us, after all. Thanks for your time, though. You've been a tremendous help in all of this.''

The entire time that Jack had been talking, he was edging Beth toward the doorway leading outside. Within moments they had made their escape. The attorney said nothing while they did. He simply watched and smiled.

Jack and Beth drove their vehicles straight to her house. Only it was *their* house now. In the near future, Jack knew that his wife would be selling his condo for him.

And this time when Jack and Beth fell into each other's arms and made mad passionate love, they knew in their hearts that whatever it was they had going for them, it was something that was going to last forever.

"I'm so in love with you, Jack," Beth said at last, after her desire for him was sated once more. She snuggled in as close to him as possible.

"Trust me, Beth," he replied. "You have my heart…my soul…my complete devotion. You are the very air I breathe. For as long as I live, I promise I'll be here for you."

And Beth knew without a doubt that he would be.

He was, after all, her most devoted, her most trustworthy friend in the whole wide world.

He always had been.

He always would be.

At long last, her dreams were coming true.

And the best part of it all was, the fact that she and Jack had been such good friends first, before the loving, and were still such good friends now, after the loving, made her feel secure in her marriage in a way she had once thought impossible.

She was, indeed, completely happy.

She was, in fact, a woman in love.

*   *   *   *   *

Modern Romance™
...seduction and
passion guaranteed

Tender Romance™
...love affairs that
last a lifetime

Sensual Romance™
...sassy, sexy and
seductive

Blaze
...sultry days and
steamy nights

Medical Romance™
...medical drama on
the pulse

Historical Romance™
...rich, vivid and
passionate

29 new titles every month.

*With all kinds of Romance for
every kind of mood...*

MILLS & BOON®

Makes any time special™

MAT4

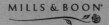

MILLS & BOON®

Tender Romance™

THE ENGAGEMENT EFFECT- Two brand-new tantalising stories...

An Ordinary Girl by Betty Neels

When Professor James Forsyth meets Philomena Selby
it's love at first sight. James is determined to convince
Philly *she'll* be the only wife he'll ever have.

A Perfect Proposal by Liz Fielding

Wasn't it madness to marry your secretary to provide a
baby with a mother? Jane, Mark's secretary, didn't think
so; but she wanted a marriage for love—not convenience.

THE ENGLISHMAN'S BRIDE by Sophie Weston

Sir Philip Hardesty, UN negotiator, is famed for his cool
head. But for the first time in his life this never-ruffled
English aristocrat is getting hot under the collar—over a
woman! Kit Romaine is not easily impressed—if Philip
wants her he's going to have to pay!

THE BRIDEGROOM'S VOW by Rebecca Winters

Millionaire Dimitrios Pandakis has vowed that he will
never be trapped into marriage. And he has been so true
to his word that despite his reputation as a heartbreaker
he has yet to take a woman to bed! But Alexandra
Hamilton has somehow worked her way under his skin...

THE WEDDING DARE by Barbara Hannay

As chief bridesmaid Laura has certain duties on her best
friend's hen night—like picking up the evening's
entertainment, a male stripper! But, Laura has hijacked
respectable single dad Nick Farrell, for whom taking his
clothes off in public is out of the question...

On sale 1st February 2002

*Available at most branches of WH Smith,
Tesco, Martins, Borders, Eason, Sainsbury's
and most good paperback bookshops.*

Treat yourself this Mother's Day to the ultimate indulgence

3 brand new romance novels and a box of chocolates

= only £7.99

Available from 18th January

2 FREE

books and a surprise gift!

We would like to take this opportunity to thank you for reading this Mills & Boon® book by offering you the chance to take TWO more specially selected titles from the Tender Romance™ series absolutely FREE! We're also making this offer to introduce you to the benefits of the Reader Service™—

- ★ FREE home delivery
- ★ FREE gifts and competitions
- ★ FREE monthly Newsletter
- ★ Exclusive Reader Service discount
- ★ Books available before they're in the shops

Accepting these FREE books and gift places you under no obligation to buy, you may cancel at any time, even after receiving your free shipment. Simply complete your details below and return the entire page to the address below. *You don't even need a stamp!*

YES! Please send me 2 free Tender Romance books and a surprise gift. I understand that unless you hear from me, I will receive 4 superb new titles every month for just £2.49 each, postage and packing free. I am under no obligation to purchase any books and may cancel my subscription at any time. The free books and gift will be mine to keep in any case.

N2ZEA

Ms/Mrs/Miss/Mr ....Initials.....................................
BLOCK CAPITALS PLEASE

Surname ....

Address ....

....

....Postcode..............................

Send this whole page to:
UK: FREEPOST CN81, Croydon, CR9 3WZ
EIRE: PO Box 4546, Kilcock, County Kildare (stamp required)

Offer valid in UK and Eire only and not available to current Reader Service subscribers to this series. We reserve the right to refuse an application and applicants must be aged 18 years or over. Only one application per household. Terms and prices subject to change without notice. Offer expires 30th April 2002. As a result of this application, you may receive offers from other carefully selected companies. If you would prefer not to share in this opportunity please write to The Data Manager at the address above.

Mills & Boon® is a registered trademark owned by Harlequin Mills & Boon Limited.
Tender Romance™ is being used as a trademark.